DRAGONFELL

DRAGONFELL

SARAH PRINEAS

HARPER

An Imprint of HarperCollins*Publishers*

Library of Congress Cataloging-in-Publication Data

Names: Prineas, Sarah, author.
Title: Dragonfell / Sarah Prineas.
Description: First edition. | New York, NY : Harper, an imprint of
    HarperCollinsPublishers, [2019] | Summary: "When a factory
    owner comes to Rafi's village and accuses the boy of being
    'dragon-touched,' Rafi sets off on an adventure to save his home
    and discover the truth about dragons, and himself"
    —Provided by publisher.
Identifiers: LCCN 2018025424 | ISBN 9780062665553 (hardback)
Subjects: | CYAC: Dragons—Fiction. | Adventure and
    adventurers—Fiction. | Fantasy.
Classification: LCC PZ7.P93646 Dr 2019 | DDC [Fic]—dc23
LC record available at https://lccn.loc.gov/2018025424

Typography by Andrea Vandergrift
19 20 21 22 23   PC/LSCH   10 9 8 7 6 5 4 3 2 1

❖

First Edition

For my mighty mother, Anne Bing,
with love

CHAPTER 1

If I stand at the very edge of the high fell that overlooks my village, and the wind is bright and cold, and I lean forward just a bit . . .

And *just* a bit more so that the wind is holding me up . . .

It feels like flying.

And then my foot slips and I almost *am* flying. Falling, I mean. I totter for a second on the edge, and with a whirl of my arms I catch my balance. That was close. I would've fallen a long way, that's for certain sure, before I hit the ground.

The day is fine and bright, the blue sky scudding with clouds, the grass on the hills holding on to a last smudge of green before winter. The chilly wind blows right through me, but I'm not cold.

I am never cold.

I have very keen eyes for things that are far away, and from up here on the Dragonfell I can see my village, a little cluster of cottages and smoky chimneys clinging to the steep slopes of the fell. Over it all the morning light flows as sweet and golden as honey.

Clouds race overhead, casting the village in shadow, and then the sun flashes out again. It's followed by a gust of wind that rushes past, and just for a moment I want to leap in the air and rush after it.

A long time ago, they say, a dragon had its lair up here on the high fells. Stepping back from the edge of the cliff, I crouch and poke around in the packed dirt, and pry up a corner of a smashed teacup about the size of my big toe. I spit on it and rub some of the dirt away with my finger. It shines in the sunlight, and I can see a tiny blue flower like a star painted on it. Standing, I put it into my pocket. The whole top of the fell is littered with shards like this. The dragon who lived up here hoarded fine teacups and sugar pots and teapots and cream pitchers, all painted with blue flowers. The broken pieces are the only thing left of the dragon, that and some old gnawed sheep bones.

What was it like for the dragon, living up here with its teacup hoard and the wind and the cold? Maybe it sat up here just like I do, looking over the high, rolling fells and the village.

Yesterday Tam Baker's-Son told me that his da told him not to talk to me anymore. Not to be unneighborly, he said, just to keep his distance.

It's a bitter thought, knowing my friend isn't my friend anymore. Tam's da said what he did because of the wild fire-red hair that I have, and my dark eyes, and because I spend too much time up here on the Dragonfell. Tam once said that he didn't know how I could see out of my eyes because they were so full of shadows. And my face is sharp, Tam says, and too fierce. Still, I've lived here all my life, and you'd think people would've gotten used to me by now.

Lately there's an edge on the way people look at me, as if the things that make me different also make me dangerous or bad. It worries my da, and his worry adds to my restlessness until there's nothing I can do but go rambling on the high, windy fells, talking to a dragon that isn't here anymore, and coming home after dark, feeling half wild and as hungry as a wolf.

From up here on the fell I can see our cottage at the edge of the village, where Da is working at his loom, weaving fine cloth. Below it, the road leads down into the valley, and to the city of Skarth, which is a darkness and a smudge of smoke on the horizon.

Something is moving way down the road.

A squint and a blink, and I bring it into focus. A man and a woman, it looks like. Climbing toward the village. Strangers.

We don't often get strangers coming to our village. I don't like the looks of them.

I step back from the rocky edge and head down the worn path that winds from the top of the Dragonfell, through the sheep pastures, along the stream that rushes by the village, on the steep road that goes through the village itself, and running now, I reach our cottage. Like all the village cottages it's whitewash over old stone, thatched with reeds, and it has a stone wall around a yard with a low shed in it for our goats and chickens.

As I come panting up to our front gate, I see my da standing in the doorway talking to the strangers. He's leaning heavily on his crutch. My da's a tall, strong man, but he's got a withered leg, burned in a fire a long time ago, and he can't get around very well.

The man he's talking to is ordinary. He has a round hat and a bushy black mustache and he has arms so long they practically hang down to his knees. The woman, though—she is like nobody I've ever seen before. She has shaved-short grizzled hair and she's tall—even taller than my da—and she's wearing rough clothes and boots with steel caps on the toes. Her eyes are hidden behind a pair of smoked-lens spectacles. That's not the strangest thing about her, though. The strangeness is the pins. She has row upon row of straight pins stuck in the lapels of her coat. Safety pins of all sizes dangle and jingle from the edges of her sleeves. She has a row of pins stuck through each one of her ears, and two pins in her left eyebrow, and one little brass pin in her *nostril*.

As I come up, the man is saying something, and Da braces himself in the doorway as if he's expecting a blow. These bristle-pin, steel-toed, long-armed strangers are a threat, and they're more than he can manage.

But me—I can manage them.

At the gate, I bounce on my toes, feeling brimful of energy, as if I'm not made of muscle and bones, but of sparks barely contained inside me. When I look at the strangers, it's like they're at the other end of a long tube—they seem tiny, as if I could take a single bound and have them at my feet, howling with terror. At the same time, I feel something in my chest, right beside my heart. I've only felt it twice before. It's an odd kind of click, like when you scrape a tinder against a flint and a bit of flame leaps up. It makes me feel shaky and hollow, and it makes me feel bold, too. As the spark inside me flares, I open the gate and go into the yard.

"It would be a shame," the pin woman is saying to Da, "if a fine weaving loom like yours was to get burned."

My da frowns. He doesn't like fire.

"But with that kind of thing in your village . . . ," the woman continues, her voice rough. She shrugs. "Tell him, Stubb."

The long-armed man strokes his mustache. "Ah, I'll tell you what, Weaver. Bad, burning trouble is what it means."

My da opens his mouth to say something, and then he sees me at the gate. He straightens and speaks past the two strangers. "Go inside, Rafi," he orders.

He's trying to protect me. "No, Da." I'm not leaving him to deal with these two and their talk about burning.

The strangers turn.

Seeing me, Stubb elbows the pin woman in the ribs and says out of the side of his mouth, "Look, Gringolet. Is that . . . ?"

"Shut up," she says sharply. Then she steps closer and studies me carefully over the rims of her spectacles. Gringolet's eyes are cold, an ashy gray like a fire gone out. She hides them away again behind the smoked lenses and turns to my da. "This isn't your boy, is it, Weaver?"

Da's face is set like stone. "Yes, he is."

"He's an odd one," the pin woman says slowly. I can feel her ashy eyes looking me up and down again. "Quite a young *spark*, isn't he?"

"He's the one Mister Flitch—" Stubb begins.

"Shut *up*," Gringolet interrupts, and I don't see her move, but Stubb flinches and snaps his mouth closed. I catch a glimpse of a long, sharp pin in Gringolet's fingers, and then it disappears up her sleeve. She reaches up and pulls at one of the pins dangling from her earlobe. "Trouble," she says, turning to Da again. "Trouble's coming for this village."

"Burning trouble," Stubb puts in.

That is definitely a threat. In response, my fingertips tingle, and shadows gather at the edge of my vision. Nobody threatens my da. *Nobody.* "You can take your talk about burning Da's weaving loom," I tell them, "and go away."

Stubb gives a bark of scornful laughter. "It's not *us* burning any looms, boy-o. *We* aren't threat'ning, we're *warning.*"

"Sounded like a threat to me," I say in a fierce voice, and I feel the spark inside me burst into flame.

My da's eyes go wide. "Oh no," he whispers.

And then the strangers start to scream.

CHAPTER 2

"But what did you *do* to them, Rafi?" Tam Baker's-Son asks.

I glance aside at my da, who shakes his head, but won't look at me.

"It happened too fast," I say. I can still feel sparks fizzling in the tips of my fingers and in my toes, making me jumpy, and I take a deep breath to steady myself. "I don't know what I did."

"Tell it," orders Old Shar Up-Hill as she climbs onto a stone block so she can see all the villagers who have gathered in her yard. Old Shar is short and skinny and wrinkled, and she has a flock of fifty sheep that give the softest wool. She lives in the center of the village, and whenever two people have a dispute or if something needs to be decided, they take it up to Old Shar's.

"Here's what I saw," says our nearest neighbor, Lah Finethread. She's known for spinning fine, strong thread, and for weaving her straight blond hair into complicated knots and braids, *and* she's known for knowing everyone else's business. "I was coming out to feed my hens, and I saw two strangers at Jos By-the-Water's front door." Lah turns her head so that the sun glints on her golden hair. She's enjoying the attention. "They knocked and Jos stepped out, and they seemed to be talking. And *then*—" She pauses and looks around to be sure everyone's listening.

"Then what happened, Lah?" asks John Smithy in his deep voice.

Everyone leans forward, keen to hear Lah's answer. "*Then* a cloud crossed the sun and all went dark," she says. "Rafi came storming across the yard, surrounded by shadows and sparks—and then he smote the strangers with a bolt of flame."

"*Smote?*" I exclaim, and I almost feel like laughing, even though it isn't funny. "It didn't happen that way at all."

"I'm telling you what I saw!" our neighbor Lah protests.

"Go on," Old Shar orders.

"And *the-e-en*," Lah says slowly, drawing everyone's

attention back to herself. "Then I felt a scorching blast of wind, and I saw the thatch on Jos By-the-Water's cottage burst into flame! *Then*, while the two strangers were screaming and running away, I saw Rafi there—" She points at me—"reach up with his bare hands and pull down the burning thatch."

"I saw Rafi do that once, too," puts in Tam Baker's-Son unexpectedly. Everyone turns to stare at him, and he flushes. "Not too long ago I was coming up to Jos's cottage and looked in at the door," he says quickly. "I saw Rafi reach right into the fire and touch the coals. I didn't say anything about it then, because I thought I'd seen it wrong."

"Without scorching his fingers?" Old Shar asks.

Tam shrugs and casts me a half-apologetic look. "It didn't seem to. It's why I guessed I must've seen it wrong."

"Rafi, show your hands," Old Shar orders.

I hold out my hands and the villagers edge closer to look. The cuffs of my shirt are charred black from the fire, and my fingers are smudged with smoke, but my hands are unscarred, unburned.

"I work at the forge all day, and I know what flames should do," John the blacksmith says. He holds up his hand to show the scars from burns that cross his dark skin, and then he points at my hands. "That's wrong, it is."

When I glance at him, he flinches back as if he's just touched molten-hot metal. "All I did," I explain, "was put out a fire that would have burned our cottage down."

"But there was that other time," Jemmy says. He looks around at the villagers. "Remember?" They all nod.

That other time was two years ago in the early spring, and rain had been falling for ten days without stopping, until icy waterfalls were streaming down the sides of the high fells. In the middle of a sleety downpour, a sheep and her twin lambs went missing. Half the village was out looking, but I was the one who found them.

Here's the thing about sheep. They are stupid. The mother sheep—the ewe—had led her two newborn lambs into a little cave in the hillside, and they'd gotten stuck there when a waterfall started pouring down in front of it. When I found them, the lambs were up to their bellies in icy water, and all three of them were just about frozen. So I got in there with them, and that's when I felt my spark flare up.

When the villagers found us, the cave was warm and dry and steam was rising off the lambs' wool.

Everybody started looking at me differently after that.

They liked that I had saved the ewe and her lambs. They just didn't like how I'd done it.

The second time I felt the spark, I was up on the Dragonfell as the sun was setting, when four wolves came from the highest fells and got in among the sheep. I raced down, and as I chased them away my spark burst into flame.

Old Shar was there—it was her sheep the wolves were after—and she saw me, and she gave me a talking-to.

Things are hard, Rafi, she said as we stood there on the hillside with the nighttime shadows gathering around us. *The factory mills in Skarth run day and night, making cotton cloth that is far cheaper than the fine woolen cloth that we make here. If people don't buy our cloth, the village will die.*

I wasn't sure what that had to do with the wolves in the sheep.

Listen, Old Shar said impatiently. *You're different from the rest of us, Rafi, and not just in your looks and your restlessness. Now there's this spark in you, these flames. In good times that wouldn't be such a bad thing, but right now the entire village is frightened of how the world is changing. And when people are afraid, they lash out at whoever they can see to blame.* She nodded at me. *That's you. You must try, Rafi, not to be so different.*

I did try. But the spark is in me. I can't put it out.

All the villagers, people I've known since I was a tiny baby, are staring at me, and muttering, and a few of them even look a little afraid of me.

"All right, all right," Old Shar says sharply, and bangs

her shepherd's crook twice on the stone block. "I will deal with Rafi. The rest of you, go home."

Grumbling, the villagers go out of Old Shar's yard and head to their sheep or back to weaving and spinning.

With a nod to Old Shar, Da gives my shoulder a squeeze, and he turns to make his slow, unsteady way back down the hillside to our cottage.

"Well, Rafi?" Old Shar asks, climbing down from the block of stone. "How much of what Lah Finethread says she saw really happened?"

"There wasn't any smiting, I'll tell you that much," I say.

"Is that so?" Old Shar replies, frowning at me. "Because those strangers came to my door, too. They're looking for something." She reaches into her apron pocket and pulls out a piece of paper. After unfolding it, she hands it to me.

Without looking at it, I hand it back.

Of all the kids in the village, I am the stupidest. The words in books never say anything to me. I can't read and I can't write, and Old Shar, who is our teacher, knows it.

"Don't you glare at me, Rafi," Old Shar says, and gives me the paper again. "Look at it."

Squinting, I examine the paper. There are words, which I don't bother with, but above them I can make out a picture. It's a blurry sketch of a house with orange-painted flames coming out of the windows and the front door.

Old Shar taps the paper. "This Gringolet person told me that there have been fires set in villages near here. Many weaving looms have been burned. People are having to leave their homes and go down to Skarth to work in the factory mills."

When I speak, I can barely get the words out. "Th-that's what they were saying to Da. That his loom would be burned."

"That's what they said to me, too," Old Shar says. Then she adds something unexpected. "Show me what's in your pockets."

I blink and then pull out the shard of teacup with the blue flower on it that I found on the fell above the village.

Old Shar nods and waves the paper at me. "The person they're looking for, this says, the one who set the fires, might be strangely interested in dragons."

"Dragons," I repeat.

"You do spend a lot of time up on the Dragonfell," Old Shar points out.

I shove the shard of teacup back into my pocket. "I did not burn any looms, Old Shar, and you know it."

Old Shar sighs and leans against her crook. "Yes, I

know it wasn't you. I will speak to Gringolet and Stubb the next time they come. And you—" She fixes me with her keen eyes. "You go on home. And Rafi, you stay out of trouble if you can."

I go. But I know that trouble is going to find me, whether I like it or not.

CHAPTER 3

My da's never been much of a talker. Sometimes there's hardly a word between us from morning to night. There's just the constant sound of his weaving loom, the shuttle going *swath* across the warp and *whirr* as the thread spins out from the bobbin, and *thump-thump* as he sends the shuttle whirring back again.

The loom that does Da's talking for him is a square frame made of heavy wood, and it fills half of the one main room of our cottage. Da keeps his back to the room as he weaves, his broad, bony shoulders hunched, his big hands busy with the shuttle.

It's just me and Da. My ma's been gone since I was born. Da never talks about her.

Swath and *whirr* and *thump-thump* wake me in the

morning. It's Da's way of saying *Get up, Rafi, go milk the goats and make breakfast.*

Up on my sleep shelf, I lie as still as I can—which isn't very still—and blink at the thatched roof overhead. My fingers and toes tingle. Scraps of a roiling dream blow out of the corners of my mind—the strangers from the day before mixed up with wind and flame and bits of broken teacups. My throat is sore. I feel like I was gargling fire all night.

Swath, whirr, thump-thump.

"All right, Da," I croak. Quickly I hop out of bed, pull on my shirt and pants, then climb down the ladder.

Our cottage has a front door and a back door and just the one window, which is right beside the loom so Da will have enough light to work by. The rest of the dim main room has a wooden table and chairs, a hearth, and a cupboard that holds some food, a few plates, a dented pot, and a pan.

I pause at the bottom of my sleep-shelf ladder. The stone floor feels cold under my bare feet, but cold never bothers me.

The *whirr* of the loom falls silent, and Da turns on the bench to look at me. "Mornin', Rafi," he says.

I take the two steps to him and lean into his shoulder, and he kisses the top of my head. "Mornin', Da," I say, and I wait to see if he has more to say.

You slept well during the night? he could ask.

Yes, Da, I would tell him, *except I had that dream again, and I keep thinking about what happened with those strangers.*

Come and have breakfast and we'll talk about it, Da might say. But he doesn't.

He's quiet about most things, but the thing he *can't* talk about, not with me, not with anybody, is fire. It's because of his leg, and what happened when it was burned. I don't know the story of it; he's never told me. I don't think he's ever told anyone.

Letting me go, he turns back to his weaving. "See to breakfast," he says, and then the *whirr* of the loom begins again.

Quietly I pad over to the hearth and swing the kettle on its hook over the fire, and then, checking to be sure that Da can't see what I'm doing, I reach into the fire and poke the coals so they burn better. Tam did see me put my hand in the fire that one time, because flames don't bother me any more than cold does. Then I take the bucket and go outside.

The sun is not quite up, and my breath steams in the chilly air. New snow dusts the very top of the Dragonfell. Soon the snow will creep down the sides of the fell and start piling up in the village. Winters are hard here, and long, and hungry.

For a moment I stand and look up the road toward

the village. All seems well. Fires and lanterns are lit in the other cottages; I can taste smoke in the air, and I can hear the *clang-clang* of John Smithy already at work at his forge. No doubt he's making one of his intricate iron weather vanes. Every house in the village has one of his vanes on the peak of its thatched roof. Ours does, too. We always know which way the wind is blowing here, that's for certain sure.

Farther up the road I can see the bright blue door of Tansy Thumb the seamstress's house, which will have blue flowers and vines growing all over it in the spring-time, and the long, low cottage where Jemmy and Jeb live, singing in harmony all day while they weave cloth almost as fine as my da's, and nearly at the top of the village, the cottage and herb garden of Ma Steep, who raises herding dogs that are almost as smart as people, when it comes to sheep.

Seeing the village, my heart settles. I may be different from all of them, but my place is here. I know it, the same as I know the Dragonfell isn't ever going to heave itself up to stand on stony legs and walk away.

Crossing the yard, I go to the stream that tumbles down the hill behind our house and wash my face and take up some water into the bucket.

The sun peeks over a distant hill, and the frost along the edge of the stone wall sparkles in the new light, and a swirl of wind rushes past the cottage, and for just a moment I want to leap into the air and rush after it.

With the wind, and with all that happened yesterday, it's a restless day for certain sure. A day for the clear cold air up on the high fells, and finding bits of broken teacups, and talking to a dragon that isn't there.

But Da doesn't like me going up to the Dragonfell.

When I open the door to the shed, our four chickens bustle out, clucking, and start pecking at the dirt in the yard. I slip inside and go to the goats' pen. Pet is an old nanny who still gives a little milk; she blinks and says *maaaaah*. The other goat, Poppy, is small and fat and she's the color of cinnamon, with a white nose and black legs and a narrow black stripe next to each eye. As soon as I step into the pen, Poppy hustles over and leans against me, warm and heavy; her fur prickles against my legs. I give them some hay and water, and while they eat I milk them.

As I milk Poppy, she looks over her shoulder at me. Her eyes are strange—even stranger than mine—golden with a sideways slit for a pupil, but her face seems happy and calm as I talk to her.

When the bucket is full of milk, I duck into the house, where I cook eggs and cheese for breakfast, leaving Da's plate on the table for him. Then I go out our front gate and head up the road toward the village.

None of the other villagers ever talk about the dragon who lived up on the Dragonfell with its teacup collection. It's been gone for such a long time. But Old Shar was right about me. I've always been *strangely interested* in dragons. Now I'm even more interested in them. And Old Shar can tell me more.

One windy day last spring when I was coming down from the highest fells, Old Shar called me over to help her, and I asked what it was like in the village when the dragon still lived here.

Old Shar was kneeling beside one of her sheep, putting medicine on its hoof while I held its head. She paused, and her eyes got a faraway look. "When I was a girl, we had a kind of festival about this time of the year. We would go up and leave the dragon a present, and it would keep the wolves away from the flocks and lambs. It was always there, like part of the fells."

"Are there dragons in other places?" I asked. My head felt funny asking that question. The village was my whole world; I wasn't used to thinking about anywhere else.

Old Shar nodded. "I hear they tell stories about a dragon in Barrow, a town about three days walk over the fells, then along the river."

"Will our dragon ever come back?" I asked.

Old Shar shook her head. "The world is changing,"

she said. "With all the factories and steam engines and roads, there's no room in it any more for dragons. The one in Barrow might not be there anymore." She inspected the sheep's hoof and then climbed to her feet. "You can let her go." I did, and we stood and watched the sheep hobble off. "Some people say," Old Shar went on, "that dragons were greedy thieves. The people down in Skarth, in the city, they tell stories about how every dragon steals and hoards a different thing, like jewels or crowns or princesses." She bent and picked up her shepherd's crook. "Some people say we're better off without dragons."

"What do *you* think?" I asked her.

She turned and looked up at the highest fell, where the dragon used to live. Her eyes got that faraway look again. "Ah, Rafi, the dragon was so beautiful when it flew. It would launch itself from up there, and open its wings, and the sound was like thunder. Then a rush of wind, and it would swoop and circle, with the sun glinting on its scales. Our dragon was bluer than the sky, and it shimmered when it flew." She shook her head, and her eyes cleared. "Our dragon was dangerous, there's no doubt about that. But it kept watch up there. It kept us safe. The dragon was our protector."

CHAPTER 4

When I've almost reached the gate outside Old Shar's house, I see Tam Baker's-Son leading his donkey down the steep road. Tam, who used to be my friend but isn't anymore. After yesterday, he certain sure isn't going to talk to me.

As he comes closer, he stares.

It's a frosty morning, and he's wearing warm clothes and shoes, and knitted woolen mittens on his hands. I have those things, but I don't feel the cold, and I forgot to put them on. All I've got on is my usual shirt and trousers and bare feet.

"Mornin', Tam," I say as I pass.

Tam twitches and ducks his head. "Mornin', Rafi,"

he mutters, and tugs on his donkey's lead rope and hurries away.

With a sigh I turn and open the gate to Old Shar's yard, and see her step out of her front door. John Smithy comes out after her. I stop and stare as Gringolet, with her rows of pins and her smoked glasses, follows. And after her comes a new stranger.

He is finely dressed—more shiny and fine than anyone I've ever seen, in a fancy black suit with a fur-lined coat over it, glints of gold rings on his fingers, and polished shoes on his feet. He has a neatly trimmed white beard and a gold chain that goes from a button to a pocket in his embroidered waistcoat. His gray-green eyes are shadowed by bushy white brows. As he steps outside, his keen gaze sweeps the yard and fastens on me. His heavy brows go up, as if in surprise, and he turns to say something to Gringolet, who nods and points at me.

Closing the gate behind me, I start across the yard.

Old Shar comes to meet me. She's wearing her best blue dress and has a flowered kerchief knotted under her chin. "It's all right," she says in a low voice. "It's Mister Flitch, a factory owner from Skarth. He just wants to talk to you."

He must have sent Gringolet with the paper and the questions. He thinks I might be the one who is burning cottages and looms in other villages. "Good," I tell Old Shar, keeping my eyes on the old man. "Because I want to talk to him."

With a knobbled hand she grabs me by the shoulder, making me stop. "Be careful," she whispers as Mister Flitch comes closer. "For once, take a minute to think about what you're going to do, Rafi, before you do it."

"Oh, sure," I mutter to her, because she knows as well as I do that her good advice is impossible for me to follow.

Mister Flitch comes up to us. He's leaning on a cane with a gold head, but he doesn't seem weak or frail. With his free hand he fingers the fine gold chain at his waist. "Well, Shar Up-Hill," he begins, and his voice is deep and a little bit sneering, in a way that makes me feel prickly. "What do we have here?"

"He's just a boy from the village, Mister Flitch," Old Shar says, sounding not nearly as sharp as she usually does.

"*Is* he?" Flitch's steely eyes are studying me carefully. "And yet he sent Gringolet and Stubb running home yesterday like dogs with singed tails." Behind him, Gringolet is scowling at me. "I think he needs to tell her that he is sorry."

"They were talking about burning," I say. "Threats,

it sounded like, and my da's afraid of fire."

"That doesn't sound like an apology," Mister Flitch says.

"Because it isn't," I shoot back.

"Rafi," Old Shar warns. John Smithy has his burly arms folded and a disapproving frown on his face.

I ignore them. I have a bad feeling about Mister Flitch. He hasn't taken his eyes off me since he stepped out of Old Shar's cottage. Then he steps nearer and, leaning on his cane, peers even more closely at me, looking deep into my eyes.

I stare back at him.

"Shadows," he murmurs. "Only shadows."

Then the spark inside me flickers.

In response, his own eyes widen, and for just a flash he looks exultant, and he says in a hissing whisper, so only I can hear him, "Ah, I see it."

"What do you see?" I whisper.

"I see something that you have," he hisses back. "And I want it. If you do not give it willingly, I will take what I need from under your village."

I don't know what he means by that. Nothing is under my village except rock, and more rock. So I look deeper into him, just like he's doing to me. Inside, he's greedily, hungrily glittering.

And I see something else. He's a threat.

"If you try to hurt my village, or anybody who lives here," I tell him, "I will stop you." And I give him my fiercest glare.

He blinks, and the connection between us breaks. He straightens and looks away, and his eyes are red and watering, as if he's been looking at the sun.

"Did you hear that?" Gringolet asks, at Mister Flitch's shoulder. "*My* village, he said."

"Yes, I heard," he says impatiently.

Gringolet gives me an ashy look over the rim of her spectacles. "So interesting."

"You'll do well to watch this one," Mister Flitch says loudly. "This boy has the look of one who is dragon-touched."

"I'm *what*?" I ask.

Old Shar's eyes have gone wide. "Dragon . . . touched?"

"Yes." Mister Flitch sneers. "There's a word for it. Everyone knows that dragons are malicious, cruel creatures. In fact—" He gestures at Gringolet, who reaches into a pocket and pulls out a book about the size of her hand. "In fact, a great expert on dragons, Igneous Ratch, has written a book describing and delineating their great evil." Gringolet holds the book out to Old Shar, and after a moment, she accepts it. "In this book," Flitch goes on, "Ratch also describes certain strange people. People who are different from other humans." He points at me. "And not just in their looks. These people have . . . let us call it a depraved affinity for dragons. For a time they seem normal, and then terrible things begin to happen around them. I hear," he says, still watching me very closely, "that his cottage burst into flames yesterday, when he was nearby. Isn't that true?"

I feel the first tremor of fear. It *is* true.

"Yes, it is," Old Shar admits after a moment.

"And, lately," Flitch goes on, "there have been burnings in villages not far from here."

"Quite a coincidence," Gringolet puts in.

"But I never—" I start to protest.

"He is dangerous," Mister Flitch interrupts. "Just look at him. That hair. Those eyes. You can tell, can't you?"

John Smithy gives a hesitant nod.

"Different doesn't mean dangerous," I insist.

"This boy," Flitch goes on, as if I haven't spoken, "spends a good deal of time in the lair of the evil dragon that once inhabited the fells here, doesn't he?"

At that, John Smithy blinks. "He does," he says slowly. "Certain sure he does."

"Well," Flitch concludes, looking satisfied, "clearly that evil has rubbed off on him."

"Dragons aren't evil, and neither am I," I tell them. "There are no stories about the Dragonfell dragon ever hurting anyone." I turn to Old Shar. "You told me yourself. Our dragon was dangerous, but it was our protector, too. It kept the wolves away from the sheep. Things were better, you said, when the dragon was looking out for us."

Old Shar's answer is a concerned frown. "Rafi—" she begins.

"It's a known fact that dragons are evil," Gringolet interrupts. She points to the book that Old Shar is holding. "Says so in the book, so it must be true."

I know they're wrong, or lying, and I'm about ready to explode with fury and frustration, but for once I think first. If I fight with them, they'll just say it proves that I'm bad and dangerous.

As I stand there seething, Mister Flitch gives a smug smile, making his voice syrupy as he speaks to Old Shar. "You would be wise to give this dragon-touched boy to us."

"He needs to be locked up," Gringolet puts in. "Poor Stubb is in the hospital back in Skarth with the burns this boy gave him yesterday. He should be locked up so he can't hurt anybody else."

"You must think of the safety of your village," Mister Flitch says, and he's giving me that greedy, glittering look again.

What is it that he saw? What does he really want with me?

I can see John Smithy nodding, like he agrees that I should be locked up, but Old Shar is shaking her head. "No," she says firmly. "Rafi has lived here in this village all his life, and he is ours. If he is in trouble, we'll deal with that trouble here." She gives them a brisk nod. "Now, we appreciate the warning, but you should be on your way, back to Skarth."

"Unwise, Shar Up-Hill," Mister Flitch says sharply. "Most unwise." In an instant he is all smooth politeness again, bowing and then striding out of the yard and down the steep street, followed by Gringolet. Giving me a worried look, John Smithy leaves, too.

"You don't believe them, Old Shar?" I blurt out. "Do you? What Mister Flitch and Gringolet said about me being dragon-touched, whatever that means, and what they said about dragons?"

"Oh, Rafi," she says wearily. "I don't know." She shakes her head, and I see that her wrinkled face is tired and frightened. "All I know is that this village is in danger. And I don't know what to do about it."

CHAPTER 5

Instead of going home, I head into the hills, climbing until my muscles burn and the wind swoops past me, and the air sparkles with cold in my lungs. There are wolves up here, waiting to come ravening down on the sheep, but when I'm on the Dragonfell they stay away. This high, the grass thins until the fells turn to patches of snow and stone scoured clean by the wind. I run with it, and jump from rock to rock, until all of my fierceness and fury is run out. Then I crouch in a sheltered place out of the wind and look out over the fells and hills.

My farseeing eyes trace the road winding into the valley, and on the road I see some sort of wheeled cart without horses to pull it. It puffs out clouds of black smoke as it goes along. Mister Flitch and Gringolet must have left it and walked to the village, where the road is too steep for carts, and now they're going back to the city.

I don't know what Flitch is up to. He and Gringolet—they want me for something, but I don't know what.

Dragon-touched.

Someone touched by a dragon? But I've never even *seen* a dragon. I don't believe for a second that the Dragon-fell dragon was evil, or that its dragon-ness has somehow rubbed off on me just because I spend time up here.

My heart yearns for Da, and I wish I could talk about this with him. But his bad leg means he can't come up to the high fells. He doesn't like me coming up here, either, so he'll never sit with me in this warm spot and talk. No, Da's working at his loom. There's no better weaver in the world than my da. It's what he loves, and the cloth he makes is beautiful and strong and far better than that flimsy cotton cloth they make in Mister Flitch's factories.

Even though I'm not bothered by the cold, I shiver and wrap my arms around my knees. I stay on the Dragonfell until the sun goes down and the valley below me falls into shadow. Slowly, stiffly, I get to my feet.

Maaaaaah, I hear, and when I jerk around, our goat Poppy is standing on a nearby rock looking calmly at me. I must have left the gate open this morning, and she followed me up here. And what if she'd run away, or a wolf had gotten her? Without Poppy's milk, Da and I would be in trouble.

I head down the hill, and Poppy trots after me. It is full dark by the time we reach the village. I go into our yard and put Poppy into the shed with an armful of hay, and trying not to notice the burned thatch over the door, I slip into the house.

Swath, *whirr*, *thump-thump* goes the loom.

The door clicks shut behind me.

The loom falls silent. Da straightens his shoulders and turns on the bench to face me. He never has many words, but I always know that he's glad to see me. Tonight his face is grim.

"Sorry I'm so late, Da," I tell him.

He nods. "You were up there again, weren't you?"

"Yes," I tell him. "I needed to do some thinking."

He frowns. "John the Smith came to speak with me this afternoon." He studies me carefully, as if he's seeing me in a different way than usual. "He says Old Shar had some visitors, people from the city." He takes a breath. "John Smithy says the village thinks you're making trouble for us all."

My heart gives a hollow thump in my chest. "I'm not, Da. I'm only—"

He raises a hand to stop me. "Go and get dinner," he says.

Feeling as twitchy and on edge as I've ever felt in my life, I collect eggs and cook them with some goat cheese, and slice some bread, and pour us each a cup of goat milk. Then I go to his bench and help Da to the table. He sits hunched over his plate, not looking at me while he eats.

At last the silence gets so heavy that I can't hold it up anymore. "Da?" I ask.

He puts down his fork and rests his broad hands flat against the tabletop, almost as if he's bracing himself.

"Da—" I start, but it's hard to put into words what I've been thinking about all afternoon. "I'm not making trouble, Da," I say. "I'm not—I'm not what Mister Flitch said. I'm not dragon-touched."

When Da speaks, it's without looking up at me. His voice is low, and it trembles. "Rafi." There is a long silence. For a moment I'm half afraid that he's going to get up from the table without saying anything more. Then he takes a shuddering breath. "The dragon . . ." With a shaking finger he points in the direction of the high fells. "*That* dragon." There's an edge in his voice that I've never heard before.

He pulls his leg—the one that is withered and scarred—out from under the table and points at it. Then he points toward the high fells again.

He can't speak it, but I know what he's saying. "The

dragon burned you, Da?"

His eyes are grim. He nods.

My heart shivers in my chest. "The Dragonfell dragon?"

"Yes." The same edge is in his voice again, and I realize what it is. Hatred. He *hates* the dragon.

"That can't be right," I blurt out. Not the dragon that collected teacups with blue flowers on them and watched over the village. "Da—"

"You won't remember," he says heavily. "You were not even three years old. It was a winter night. Very late, I woke up and you were gone. I followed your tracks in the snow." He points again, toward the Dragonfell. "No one had seen the dragon for a long time, but it was there. It was . . . it was huge, and you were so small, and . . ." He swallows down the words. "I picked you up and turned to run and it came after us, and it . . ." He nods at his leg, withered and burned.

"The dragon burned you," I whisper. Goose bumps prickle over my skin. "And you never told anyone."

"Never," Da says. There is a long silence. "I couldn't . . . I told everyone that I'd spilled a kettle of boiling water down my leg. I couldn't explain any more than that. And after . . ." He shakes his head. "After it happened, the dragon went away again. But listen, Rafi. Mister Flitch is right." He pauses, and he says the next

35

words like he's choking on them. "You were in my arms when the dragon came after me. Its flames washed over me and burned me, but they washed over you, too, and you were not burned. You are what that Mister Flitch said. The dragon called you, Rafi, and you went to it. You are dragon-touched."

CHAPTER 6

Flames are never still. They flicker. And so do I.

After dinner I climb up to my sleep shelf and into bed, but I know that there won't be any sleeping for me this night. I flicker with all the things I've learned today—about Da and his burned leg, and the dragon, and Mister Flitch wanting something from me. And me, being dragon-touched. It all boils and burns inside me until I have to sit up in bed and wrap my arms around my knees to keep myself from exploding.

And then I hear something that distracts me.

Our cottage is dark. The loom is silent; Da's put out the candle and gone to bed. My ears prickle with listening.

From the direction of the village I hear the creak and

swoop of the weather vanes that are perched on top of every thatched roof. The wind is shifting.

Then I hear it again, the sound that distracted me—a scream in the distance. Quickly I pull on my clothes and scramble down the ladder. A shuffle and the tap of his crutch, and Da emerges from the darkness.

"Can you smell it?" he asks, his voice tense.

And yes, I smell it—smoke.

I help him out the door. It's midnight, no moon, and dark, except off in the distance where the village clings to the hillside there's the light of leaping flames.

"Oh no," Da breathes.

"Stay here," I tell him. "I'll go."

"No." He grips my shoulder to steady himself. "They'll need all the help they can get."

Da lurches toward the fire, his face grim and pale, and I help him up the road and into the village. The air has turned sharply colder, with an edge of iron, the taste of snow. People are coming out of their cottages, shivering and blinking in the flickery orange light. As we pass, a thatched roof bursts into flame; sparks blow past in a growing wind. We round a corner, coming to the middle of the village, when a wave of heat blasts over our heads. It's Old Shar's house, the thatched roof alight with flames that leap high into the darkness. Sparks whirl up and the fire gives a deafening roar.

From inside the house comes a high scream.

"Old Shar," Da says, staring at the cottage door. A gust of flames pants from it as if the doorway is a dragon's mouth, breathing out fire. All the other villagers are busy putting out their own fires; there's no one else to help. Da takes an unsteady step toward the cottage, leaning heavily on his crutch.

"No, Da," I gasp, and grab his arm. He's big enough to shake me off, but I hold on. "No!" I shout.

He glances down at me, his face like stone in the blurring orange light.

"Let me go, Da," I say. A glowing spark whirls past, and as he flinches I reach out to catch it, then open my hand to show him that flames can't burn my skin.

"Ah no, Rafi," he groans.

"I know fire's the one thing you're most afraid of," I tell him. "But it can't hurt me. It'll be all right." And then I race away, stumbling over the doorstep and into the burning house.

The roof overhead blazes and the heat of the fire pounds at me. Embers crumble under my bare feet. I push past the flames and step farther inside. The shelf where Old Shar keeps her books is boiling with flame; charred pages swirl through the air like black snow. Nothing I can do to save them. There's no sign of Old Shar here. Leaving the main room, I hurry down a smoke-filled hallway to a door lined with licks of fire.

"Help! Help!" cries a thin voice.

With my shoulder I push open the door. By the light of the flames, through air made wavery by heat, I see Old Shar, her white hair in a braid over her shoulder, thin and frail in a white nightgown, crouched in a corner with her arms over her head, coughing.

I am *not* going to let her die. I hurry across the room to her.

"Come on," I shout.

As I bend down, she gets a good look at my face and her eyes widen. She opens her mouth in a shrill, terrified scream that ends in a choked gasp for breath, as smoke billows around us. She tries to jerk away from me, but the smoke is too much and she collapses in a faint.

Even though I'm not much bigger than she is, I'll have to carry her out. One of her books is on the floor, as if she dropped it. I grab it and shove it into my pocket. Then, gritting my teeth, I scoop Old Shar into my arms and, my muscles quivering, I manage to stand and stagger toward the door.

The main room is a wall of fire. Trying to protect Old Shar as much as I can, I place my feet carefully, peering through the wavering flames, until I crash out the front door in a whirl of smoke and ash and sparks, and stumble farther from the heat of the fire until I run into a crowd of villagers. They stare as I push through them, away from the burning cottage, and set Old Shar on the ground and kneel next to her. She's still and limp. "Old Shar, Old Shar," I say, patting her fire-reddened face, holding her hand.

"Rafi," Tam Baker's-Son says, and points at me with a shaking finger.

I stare up at him for a moment, blinking away the shadows in my eyes, and then I feel a warm spot over my ear and reach up and put out the bit of fire that's burning in my hair. There's a patch of flame on my shirt, and I pat that out, too.

The villagers, all in their nightgowns, wide-eyed with fear, stare at me, backing away. Da's not with them. The fire might've been too much for him and he's gone home.

Our neighbor Lah Finethread is here, though. "It happened again!" she screeches.

"What?" I blink up at her, not understanding.

Old Shar's hand is still in mine; her eyes have opened. She struggles to sit up, coughing. ". . . set . . . fire," she manages to get out.

Lah Finethread gasps out a little scream, drawing everyone's attention to herself. "Rafi did this!" she shrieks. "Old Shar just said that Rafi set her house on fire!"

"No, she didn't," I protest. "I didn't!"

Then, from the flame-tinged shadows, Gringolet and Stubb stumble closer. "We saw him!" Gringolet shouts, pointing at me.

Beside her, Stubb opens his mouth and eyes wide, as if he's frightened. "Saw him!" he repeats, waving his long arms.

"What?" John Smithy cries. "What did you see?"

"That boy!" Gringolet says. Over the villagers' screams and shouts, she adds, "That boy set the fire in Shar Up-Hill's cottage!"

"Dragon-touched!" Stubb bellows. "He's infected with the dragon's evil, and he set the fire. He wants to burn this entire village to the ground!"

"No, I don't," I protest, but my voice is lost in the burning roar of the roof of Old Shar's house collapsing. A wave of heat rolls out, and Lah and Tam Baker's-Son and the other villagers flinch back.

Old Shar is trying to say something else, but doubles over, coughing. There's screaming and I hear Lah shriek my name again, and other angry, fearful voices, and all I can do is kneel there feeling like the ground is about to crumble away beneath me.

Then Old Shar grabs my arm. "Rafi," she gasps. "Not . . . you." She coughs; her eyes are red and running with tears from the smoke. The flames from her house roar behind us. "Flitch . . . must have ordered them to set the fire."

I nod, quick to understand. "Gringolet burned your cottage. She knew they'd blame me for it." I'm panting now, trying to get the words out. "Old Shar, I really am dragon-touched. My da told me. Flitch wants me for something. He'll be coming after me next." Then I have a horrible thought. I told Mister Flitch that my da is afraid of fire. He's one to use that kind of knowledge. "I have to be sure my da is all right." I start to get to my feet, but her bony hand grips my sleeve, holding me at her side.

"Wait." She coughs, her white hair straggling over her hunched shoulders. "Listen, Rafi." *Cough, cough.*

"What?" I am completely distracted. I can't wait any longer to find my da. I look wildly around. Flames and billows of smoke are still swirling from Old Shar's cottage; sparks fly on the wind like shooting stars; other thatched roofs are smoldering.

"*Listen,*" she insists, and I push away my worry to focus on her. "It would suit Flitch well to have this village burned and gone, and all of us working in his factories. I have done everything I can to keep us all safe, but it's not enough." She coughs and rubs tears from her smoke-reddened eyes. "Rafi, you must go."

I stare at her. Is she casting me out?

She's racked with another cough. "We need . . . our protector."

"Protector," I repeat, and my voice shakes.

"It's out there somewhere," she rasps out. "You are dragon-touched because you're the only one who can find it."

I shake my head, not understanding. "Old Shar, I can't—"

"Pay attention, Rafi," she interrupts, and takes my chin in her hand and makes me look right into her eyes. "You were right. Dragons are not evil. Our dragon left long ago, but we need it to come back." She lets me go as she's shaken by another cough. "You must go. Leave here. Find our protector. Find . . . our . . . dragon."

CHAPTER 7

Old Shar's words echo in my ears, but I can't think about them right now. I have to find my da before Gringolet and Stubb do.

Quickly I jump to my feet and run from the village, leaving behind the shouting and the rush of footsteps as people hurry to fill buckets with water that they fling onto the smoldering thatch of their roofs. After racing down an empty stretch of road, I catch up to Da just as he's hobbling through our front gate. He lets me help him inside our cottage, then he slams our front door and latches it. I watch him fumble in the darkness and then light a candle. Without speaking, he shuffles to the cupboard and sweeps everything from the shelf into a sack.

A pounding at our front door startles me, and I jerk around.

"We know you're in there!" Stubb shouts from outside.

Da shoves the bulging sack into my arms and pushes me toward the back door. Limping past me, he opens it and peers out into the darkness. Then he takes me by the shoulders. "They're going to see that you're blamed for the fire, Rafi. You have to get away."

"Da, *no*," I protest. "You know it wasn't me. I can't—" *leave you*, I'm going to say, but I'm interrupted by another pounding at the front door.

"We've come for your boy, Weaver!" Stubb shouts. "Mister Flitch wants him. Give him to us, or we'll burn you both out."

Da shudders with fright. "You have to go, Rafi."

And I see what I have to do. "It'll be all right, Da," I say quickly. "I'll lead them away."

The front door rattles in its frame as they start trying to kick it down.

Da pulls me close and gives me a quick, hard hug. "There is one thing I fear more than fire, Rafi." He kisses the top of my head, then shoves me outside. "You have to go. *Run!*" The door slams.

I stand there for a dazed moment, smelling smoke from the fire, hearing the angry shouts of Gringolet and

Stubb at the front door. Then I move, peering around the corner of the cottage, and I see them—two hulking black shapes holding torches with flames like flickering tongues that lick the night. They're about to touch the torches to the thatch of our cottage roof. They're going to burn Da alive in there.

"Hey!" I shout at them.

Gringolet points. "There he is!" They both start after me.

I race away from the cottage, through the back gate.

They follow, the flames of their torches streaming behind them.

I run up the path that crosses the lower hills and leads toward the Dragonfell. It grows steeper. Panting, I check over my shoulder. Their torches are bright against the night—they're still coming. My leg muscles burn and I gasp for breath.

From behind me I hear a shout—glancing back, I see them, twice as big as I am, and twice as strong, too. They're driving me on, waiting until I get too tired, and then they'll have me.

Come *on*, Rafi. Think!

I can see in the dark—they can't.

Swerving, I leave the path, stumbling over the grass and rocks and heather, climbing higher and higher. From behind I hear curses, but they keep coming. Feeling almost as if I can fly, I leap from one rocky outcrop to the next, and Gringolet and Stubb fall farther behind.

Then I leap for a rock that is like a gray island sticking out of the low bushes, and my foot slips, and I tumble into a clump of prickly furze. Seeing me fall, Gringolet shouts, and they plow through the bushes, coming closer. I pick myself up and scramble away.

At last I reach the part of the fell where the grass and furze give way to weathered stone, and the path leads along a cliff just below the dragon's lair.

That's where they catch me.

As they close in, I put my back to a wall of rock. The wind swirls around us, and their torches flare.

Gringolet watches me avidly, pacing closer. "Well, little spark boy," she says, and her voice is almost a hiss. "Now we have you."

Furious, I glare at her. "Why can't you leave me and my village alone?"

In the quivering light from the torches, Gringolet's face looks twisted. The pins in her ears glint. "You have something . . ." Now she's looking at me over the rims of her spectacles, and even in the flickering torchlight, her eyes are gray and dead. "You have something that Mister Flitch wants. And Mister Flitch *always* gets what he wants."

"I don't have anything," I protest.

Gringolet's voice turns ash-bitter. "You're *special*, boy, haven't you realized that yet?"

"Now don't give us any more trouble," Stubb orders, stepping closer, his feet sliding over the pebbly rock. His face is streaked with soot; his thick black eyebrows make his eyes look like pits of shadow.

Frantically I glance to the side, looking for a way to escape.

Gringolet sees, and shifts to block me. They step closer. Stubb reaches out with his long arms to grab me.

And that strange feeling flares up in my chest again, that scrape of tinder against flint. The spark kindles, right beside my heart. Heat sizzles just beneath my skin. Shadows and sparks gather in the corners of my eyes. I take a quick glance down at my hand, and it's my own hand, pale and smudged with soot, but then the fingers start glowing ember-red, so bright that I can see the dark shadow of my bones inside.

Gringolet pulls a long, sharp pin out of her sleeve and steps closer, and my flames respond, making heat crackle from my skin. She jerks back and barks out a curse. The torch she was holding falls, bouncing once on the stony ground and then going out.

But there's plenty of light. It's coming from *me*.

"Don't take another step!" I shout at them, and I can hear the crackle of flames in my voice.

Their eyes wide, Stubb and Gringolet back away. "Now listen," Stubb says, raising his hands as if to calm me.

"Too late," I shout, taking a step toward them. It feels as if the ground should be shaking under my feet. Clenching my fists, desperate and fierce, I lunge at them. They fall over each other, trying to get away. In their panic, the other torch falls to the ground, and I stomp on it with my bare feet until it goes out.

While Stubb and Gringolet's eyes are dazzled, I crouch, wrapping my arms around myself, willing my fire to go out. And the night goes dark.

But I can see in the dark. Quietly I slip away, leaving them behind. While they run back down to report to their master and tell my entire village what they saw me do, I climb higher and higher on the Dragonfell until I reach the rocky ledge where the dragon had its lair and its hoard of teacups. In that cold and lonely place, I find a corner out of the wind and hide, and I know they will never find me.

CHAPTER 8

I wake up in the chilly gray morning huddled on the dragon's lair with my head pillowed on my sack of food. Golden, slit-pupiled eyes are staring down at me.

With a strangled yelp, I sit up, and Poppy the goat says *maaaah* and dances back a few steps on her dainty hooves.

"What are you doing here?" I ask, and my voice scares me a little, it's so hoarse from when I roared at Stubb and Gringolet last night.

Maaaah, Poppy says, and *maaah*, and she puts her head down to nibble at a bit of lichen on the rock.

I rub the sleep from my eyes and, staying low and hidden, turn to look at what I can see from up here. The sky overhead is covered with heavy clouds. The wind blows, icy cold; a few flakes of snow sting my face. Far, far below, the village clings to the side of the hill. Smudges of sooty smoke puff from the blackened remains of Old Shar's house. Lines of smoke stream from the chimneys of the villagers' cottages, too. I can see the tiny shape of Tam Baker's-Son leading his donkey up the road.

And there's Da's cottage just outside the edge of the village. Not burned. Da is safe.

Getting to my feet, I look down at the ground I'm standing on. It's weathered gray rock, a little slick, as if the dragon's belly rested here and rubbed it smooth. Shards of teacups with blue flowers on them are scattered around.

Right here is where it happened. Here's where the dragon attacked my da. I was a baby, and he was holding me in his arms. The dragon burned him. But it didn't burn me.

Why not?

Jittery, I pace in a circle while I think it through. Why not, Rafi?

What does it *really* mean to be dragon-touched?

The dragon did something to me. It must have. That's why I can't be burned, and the cold doesn't bother me. It's why I'm so restless, and why I look so different from everybody else. It's why I can see in the dark and why I can see things that are far away. It's where the strange spark that's inside of me came from.

And I don't know for sure if dragons are evil. Old Shar says they aren't. But the Dragonfell dragon burned my da, so maybe they are. I don't *feel* evil. But I think evil people probably don't. How would I know if I'm evil or not?

Slowly I turn to look down on my village again. It seems so tiny from way up here, like I could reach out and pick it up and hold it cupped in my hands to protect it. But I can't go back there to be accused of burning Old Shar's cottage down, or captured by Gringolet to be given to Mister Flitch. And I can't stay up here, either.

Something bulky is in my pocket; I reach in and pull it out. It's Old Shar's book that I saved from burning last night. It's about the size of my hand, and twice as thick, with a cracked brown leather cover. One corner is charred from the fire. Putting it into the bag that Da gave me, I take one last look at my home. As I stand there, my feet tingling with their need to move, the clouds lower, the wind picks up, and the air grows thick with snowflakes. That's a good thing. Snow means Flitch can't get his wheeled cart up the steep roads near the Dragonfell. My village will be safe, at least for a little while.

I take a deep breath. Old Shar told me to find the dragon.

I know what I have to do. I have to go out into the

world and find out the truth about me—about what it means to be dragon-touched. And I have to find the dragon who belongs here, up on the Dragonfell.

Slinging the sack over my shoulder, I set off, feeling twitchy about what happened last night, but feeling keenly excited, too. In my entire life, I've never been farther from the village than the dragon's lair up on the fell. I may be stupid, but I'm not dumb. I've listened to people talk about the rest of the world. I know about islands and oceans and mountains, and other things like that. The world is a big place, and now I get to see some more of it.

And dragons, too, maybe.

Walking fast, I go along a high ridge that leads like a sharp backbone from the Dragonfell to another set of hills and valleys. The trail is too rocky and steep for running, and the blizzardy wind is fierce in my face, but I go as fast as I can, followed by my footprints and Poppy's hoofprints in the deepening snow.

I walk for a long time with Poppy bobbing along behind me. *Maaaah*, she says, and then a more insistent *maaah, maaah, maaah*, and I realize that the morning is well along and she hasn't been milked yet.

"Poor little goat," I tell her, and lead her into a

sheltered place between two high rocks. Da put one of our tin cups in the sack; I dig it out, and as tiny snow-flakes whirl around me, I milk Poppy and gulp down a cup full of the warm milk, and then another one, and squeeze the rest of her milk onto the ground so her udder won't dry up. "Come on," I tell her, shoving the cup back into the sack.

After trudging through the snow all day, Poppy and I spend the night high on the side of a snowy fell listening to the howl of wolves in the distance. In the morning, I set off again, heading down below the snow line to where there is brown, wiry grass.

Over the fells and along the river is what Old Shar told me about the town of Barrow, where there might be a dragon.

I shade my eyes with my hand, and with my sharp vision I can see a pale line that is a road leading along the bottom of the valley below me, and then, in the distance, a winding darker line—a river.

When I get to the road, I follow it. While walking I see lots of other travelers. Some have black hair straight as a stick, or red hair in spiraling curls, or hair in long braids with beads and bits of glass woven in; some have white or pink or light brown or deep brown skin, or freck-les covering their entire faces, and some have intricate designs inked on their hands and twining up their necks.

But none of them are like me; none have fire-red hair and shadow dark eyes. Or a spark inside that makes them dragon-touched and different.

CHAPTER 9

When night falls I make my camp well off the road. The moon rises full overhead. I pull Old Shar's book out of the bag to have another look at it.

The leather cover of the book is smooth, well worn. When I open it, the smell of smoke wafts up, reminding me of Old Shar's burning house, and the frightened stares of the villagers.

It's another strange thing about me that I can see in the dark. I can't read the words, but if I hold the book at arm's length, and squint, I can make out a blurred picture. The corner of the first page is charred and eaten away by the fire, but there's still enough of it left to see a drawing of an animal. It's a hugely evil and snaky shape, with a heavy head and a muzzle full of sharp teeth, bat-like wings, and a spiked tail, all curled around what looks like it's supposed to be a hoard of gold. A dragon.

I know what this is. It's that Igneous Ratch book that Mister Flitch gave to Old Shar. It tells about how dragons are evil and malicious. Coming from Flitch, I doubt it's a good book, but it might help with my search for the Dragonfell dragon, and it might have more in it about what it means to be dragon-touched. Problem is, I can't read it. I need to find somebody who can.

When Poppy and I get to Barrow it's a town built of brick, with a main brick-paved street wide enough for heavy wagons pulled by huge horses with hooves as big as dinner plates. The people are big, too, as if they spend all their time carrying boxes of bricks around.

After looking around for a bit, I find somebody I can talk to, an old, old woman sitting in a rocking chair on the front step of a brick house. She has no teeth, and leathery dark skin, and she's wrapped in three woolen shawls—not as finely woven as Da's cloth—and she blinks at me with eyes covered by a film of white. She talks about the weather for a bit and calls me a nice lad, and I sit on the brick step beside her chair and listen, feeling like I'm at a hearth soaking up the warmth of her company. Poppy grazes nearby. After telling me about the history of Barrow, and all of her relations going back three generations, I get my question in and she tells me that there's no dragon in Barrow, hasn't been for ten years. "It was a beauty," she adds. "Just a little bitty one, about the size of a dog, but all over green and gold. It used to fly around and perch on the roofs, and that was good luck."

"What happened to it?" I ask her.

She rocks back and forth a few times; her filmy eyes blink. "I don't rightly remember what happened. It was about the time the bosses came in with their new machines and got the brickworks started. There was a lot of talk, y'see, but nobody really knew."

"Have things gotten worse here since the dragon left?" I ask her.

She gives a little cackle. "I'm ninety-three years old, boy. Old ones like me always think things were better when we were younger." She chews the next words over for a bit, then goes on. "Now, if you want to find a dragon you should try Coaldowns. There's talk of a dragon there, an old one, an' it's giving 'em plenty of trouble, what I hear." It's four more days to Coaldowns, she tells me.

Then a younger woman comes out of the house. Eyeing me suspiciously, she helps the old woman to her feet. "Come inside, Mother," she says, as if talking to a baby. "It's time for dinner and your bath." She puts her arm protectively around the old woman and pulls her toward the door.

"Such a nice boy," the old woman says.

Because Da would expect me to be polite, I say, "Thank you," and then I try smiling at her.

The younger woman flinches, and her face, which was starting to seem friendly, turns frightened. She pulls her mother's arm. "Go on, boy. You go on away from here."

Stupid, Rafi, I tell myself as Poppy and I make our way down the street. No smiling. Keep your face still and quiet.

And there we are, me and Poppy, walking right down the main road through Barrow, staring at the sights in a town full of strangers, when I see somebody that I know.

Big man wearing a checked coat and a round hat. Stubb.

Luckily he doesn't see me. Quickly I duck into an alley between two brick houses.

Maaaah, Poppy complains.

"Shhh," I hiss at her.

Crouching, I edge around the corner, with Poppy breathing on the back of my neck, and I watch Stubb go on down the street. At the end of it he meets up with somebody else I know—Gringolet. She looks ashy gray as usual, and sort of starved and fierce. She's added more pins to the front of her coat.

At the sight of them, the spark inside me flickers. I tamp it down. I know what they're doing here. Mister Flitch has sent them out to hunt for me. It's pure stupid luck they didn't see me.

They say something to each other, and then Gringolet snatches a bag from Stubb and steps up to the wall of a tavern. Then she takes out a hammer and a few tacks and she posts a piece of paper with a picture on it and writing. Stowing the hammer in a bag, they go into the tavern.

"Wait here," I tell Poppy.

Maaah, she says, and follows as I dart out of the alley and over to the tavern wall, where I rip down the paper that Stubb and Gringolet posted, and hurry away while trying to get a look at it. There are words that I can't read, and right in the middle is a smudgy picture of a boy who must be me, looking all squinty-eyed and evil.

I can guess what the words on the paper say. It's what I thought—Flitch is after me. He's a powerful man, a factory owner. All Gringolet has to do is post papers like this and tell people to watch for a kid with fire-red hair and shadow eyes, and they'll have me.

To be safe, I switch to traveling only at night, sleeping under bushes during the daytime. As I walk toward Coaldowns, the land changes and the weather gets colder, and the wind smells like snow; the hills grow lower, and they are studded with black rocks, not the weathered gray I'm used to. There aren't any sheep on these hillsides, not like at home.

With every step I get farther away from my village.

I've heard the word *homesick* before, but I didn't really understand what it meant. There's a sad, echoing place growing inside me from missing Da and our cottage and the village. If I was at home, Da would notice how ragged I'm getting and he'd give Tansy Thumb a length of fine-woven woolen cloth to stitch a new shirt for me. He'd remind me to put on my shoes, too, now that it's winter. I miss my cozy sleep shelf and the *whirr* and *thump-thump* of Da's loom. I even miss the way our chickens look so offended when I reach into their nests to take their eggs.

CHAPTER 10

"Dirty beggars isn't welcome here," says an old Coal-downs man with a wrinkled face and brown teeth. He's a guard, he tells me, and it's clear Flitch's hunters haven't been here yet, because he's only ordinarily suspicious, not on the lookout for a *dragon-touched boy*. "Go on back where you come from," he says, "or you'll end up a pro-pitiation like the last beggar to come through here." He moves to stand, blocking a narrow street leading into the town.

We don't have any beggars in our village, and I don't know what a *propitiation* is. "I'm not begging for any-thing," I tell him.

"You sure do look like a beggar," he says, and folds

his arms across his skinny chest. "'Tis a town rule. No vagrants, tramps, lunatics, scroungers, idiots, tinkers, or dirty beggars allowed, punishable by designation as a propitiation."

I point to Poppy. "I have a goat. What kind of beggar has a goat with him?"

He shrugs. "A beggar with a goat, is what. *And* you don't look right. You isn't coming in."

Glaring at him won't work, and neither will smiling, so I turn and walk back along the road leading out of Coaldowns until I find a stream to wash my face. It's bitter cold, but the spark of heat in my chest keeps me warm as I wade in and then stick my head underwater. All cleaned up, I put my hand on Poppy's neck and try another road leading into the town. This time when a different town guard stops me, I keep my head down and lie. "I'm taking this goat to the market," I say, and she lets me pass.

Coaldowns is a grim, bleak place. All around its edges are hill-sized piles of black and gray stone shards. Inside the town, everything is built of dark gray slate, from the narrow streets, to the rows of blank-fronted houses, to the steep-slanted roofs. It's all stained with sooty black, and the air is thick with a strange-tasting smoke. In the distance is the roaring sound of metal gears and clanking.

The one or two people we pass have suspicious eyes; as Poppy and I walk through the streets, they watch, silent.

A shrieking whistle sounds, and the streets grow crowded with people carrying baskets to the market-place, and workers covered with black coal dust making their way home.

None of them will talk to me.

And I'm running out of time. Gringolet and Stubb can't be too far behind.

Maaaah, Poppy says, so I find a narrow alley between two tall stone houses, pull the tin cup out of my sack, crouch down, and start milking.

I look up to see a scrawny boy standing at the mouth of the alley peering in at us. He's a bit younger than I am, and wears a leather helmet and filthy black clothes. His blue eyes are very pale in his soot-covered face. He looks hungry.

"My goat has plenty of milk," I tell him. "Do you want some?"

The pale eyes squint. "Huh?"

He can't see me very well because I'm in the shadows of the alley, so maybe my strangeness won't frighten him. I hold up the brimming cup of milk. It's already got particles of soot floating in it, I notice. "See? Milk."

The boy nods, edges into the alley, grabs the cup, and

gulps down the milk. "Ta," he says, handing me the cup and turning to go.

"Do you want some more?" I ask, already squeezing more milk into the cup.

"Aye," the boy says, and leans against the alley wall as if he's very tired.

"Been working?" I ask him as I milk. Poppy blinks her golden eyes and watches the boy.

"Aye," the boy says again. "I work over 't the mine. We dig coal for the factories. Been under since before day."

"Under?" I ask, and hand him the cup.

"Aye. Underground. Workin'." He takes a big gulp, then burps. "That's good milk. Ta very much." He drinks some more.

I half don't even want to bother asking about dragons, because what would a dragon be doing near a cold, slate-stone, coal-digging town like this? Poppy pushes her nose against the back of my knee. "All right," I tell her. "I'm looking for dragons," I tell the boy. "Is there a dragon here?"

"Aye," he says, not even surprised by the question.

For a moment I just stare at him. "There really is?"

"Aye." The boy points. "That way, deeper in the slickens and mullock heaps." He pauses and rubs the back of his hand against his mouth, leaving a cleaner patch behind. "You a beggar?"

"I know I look like one," I say, "but I'm not."

He leans closer, as if sharing a secret. "You'll want to be careful, looking like a beggar as you do, an' askin' about the dragon. They'll take you for a propitiation, even though they've just done one."

"What is that?" I ask. "What's a propitiation?"

He shrugs. "The mineworks keep burning. They think it's the dragon that's starting the fires there. The propitiation is like a present for the dragon, making it stay away." He gives me a nod, hands me the empty cup, and heads out of the alley.

While we were talking, the streets have grown quiet again. I slip through the shadows and outside the town into the hills of stone—the mullock heaps and slickens, the boy called them. They are huge humped heaps lit here and there by smoldering orange fires. The air is smoky. I clamber up the side of one slicken and slither down the other side. The sky grows dark with clouds, as if icy rain will start falling at any moment. Here and there are pools of water colored poisonous green, with curds of white foam around their edges. Poppy sniffs at the water, but doesn't drink, and neither do I. After a while, the smoky air gets into my lungs, making me cough. I wipe a hand across my face and it comes away black with soot; I must be covered with it, just like the miner boy I met in town. Even Poppy's cinnamon-colored fur is dusted with soot.

At last we reach the base of the tallest mullock heap, three times as high and big as any of the others.

Here. This is where I will find the dragon.

A path zigzags back and forth across the steep face of the hill. People have climbed up here before. The townspeople doing their *propitiation*. Giving the dragon a present, just as the villagers in the Dragonfell used to give their dragon blue-painted teacups. Fingering the shard of teacup that I still have in my pocket, I climb the path, the sharp rocks slithering away under my feet and clattering down the steep slopes. Poppy follows, her little hooves sure on the slippery rocks. It's something I've noticed about goats: if they have the choice to walk on hard stone or on soft grass they'll choose the stone every time. They like it.

Finally we reach the top.

The darkening clouds press down from overhead. Behind them, the sun is starting to set. I can't see any dragon. It's like a wide hilltop up here, almost as big as the Dragonfell. Half of the top of the hill is gouged away to form a deep, shadowy cave made of rock shards. Tendrils of smoke drift out of the cave's mouth. The dragon must be in there. In the wide, flat, gray space

before the cave, about ten paces away from me, is a tumble of slicken with bigger, whitish-looking round stones,
and sticking up in the middle of that is a wooden post.

Tied to the post is a girl.

CHAPTER 11

She is the propitiation, I understand at once. The towns-people caught a beggar and put her up here to make the dragon stop breaking the mineworks—that's what the miner boy told me.

Is the dragon supposed to *eat* her?

My heart pounds. Maybe this proves that dragons really *are* evil.

The girl tied to the post has her head lowered, her eyes closed. She has shaggy, curly black hair, light brown skin, and she's wearing an overlarge black coat and boots that look like they might be too big for her. She hasn't seen me yet.

I don't want to startle her. And I don't want to alert

the dragon to the fact that I'm here. Slowly I slide a foot over the rocky ground. Then I take another quiet step toward her.

Maaaaah! Poppy says loudly.

At the post, the girl's head jerks up. Seeing me, she brightens. "Hello there!" she calls in a dry, cracked voice. She has hazel eyes and a splash of freckles across her nose. Her clothes—shirt and trousers under the coat—are made of well-woven cloth. She's about the same age as me, and she seems completely ordinary.

"Are you here to rescue me?" she asks.

"I—I think so," I say, not wanting to tell her that I really came here to see the dragon. With an eye on the cave, I step closer to the post. Poppy follows.

"Good!" The girl squirms a bit. "Mainly you'll have to get these ropes off." Her arms are bound to her sides; the ropes go around her, tying her to the post. "I've had the *worst* itch on my nose." She scrunches her face up. "Would you mind terribly scratching it for me?"

She's tied to a post in front of a dragon's lair and she wants me to scratch her nose?

She nods at Poppy. "That's a very nice goat you've got there. Does he follow you around? My name is Mad—um, it's Maud, I mean."

Mad Maud. That sounds about right.

"Apparently I've been offered as a particularly fine propitiation for the dragon." With her chin, she points at the cave.

I glance at it, keeping my face turned away from her. "Is it in there?"

"'Course it is!" she exclaims, not seeming at all frightened. "Though it hasn't shown any interest in me so far." She sounds almost disappointed. "Are you interested in dragons?"

"Yes," I answer. Overhead, thunder grumbles and the clouds grow even heavier. I set down my bag and rummage inside for the knife Da put in for cutting the bread. Taking it out, I step closer and examine the ropes tying her to the post. They are as thick as my wrist and knotted tightly. Those townspeople weren't taking any chances on Mad Maud escaping. I start sawing at the ropes with my bread knife.

While I'm doing that, Maud squirms around to look at me.

"Hold still," I say.

She's staring. "You have the most unusual eyes I have ever seen."

This is the point at which most people start getting scared of me, so I grit my teeth and keep working on the rope. My shoulders tense as I wait for her to shriek like Lah Finethread.

She leans forward to peer into my face. "The whites are ordinary, but the centers are so dark. How does the light get in? Do you have trouble seeing at night?"

I glance up at her, then away again. "No." I could tell her that I can see in the dark, but I don't want her to get excited about it.

"How did your hair get that bright fire color?" she asks.

Grrr, I think. *Quit looking at me, Mad Maud.* A strand of the rope parts under the knife. "This is going to take a while."

"Oh, drat," she says with a sigh. She peers at me again. "I suppose you're wondering how I got here."

"You're not a beggar," I say.

"*Obviously* I'm not a beggar," she sniffs. "I'm a scientist."

"What's a scientist?" I ask, sawing away at the rope. It's almost like wood, it's so thick and strong. A quick glance over my shoulder shows that the dragon is still in its cave.

"A scientist is somebody who gathers information and then tries to make sense of it," she answers.

"Uh-huh," I say, not quite believing her.

She chatters on. "Yes, like you, I'm very interested in dragons—I'm studying them, actually—and so I came here, and let me tell you!" she says, opening her eyes wide. "These Coaldowns people do not like it when strangers come into their town asking questions!"

"I can believe that," I say. Just a few more strands and the rope will be cut.

"So as it happens," she goes on, "I was asking a few simple questions, really not making a nuisance of myself at all, and yesterday morning they—Oh!" She interrupts herself and looks toward the cave. "Here's the dragon now. Hello!" she calls.

Maaaaah! Poppy says.

I whirl to face the cave, the knife in my hand.

Slowly the dragon emerges into the stormy gray light.

Mister Flitch wants us to think that dragons are huge, cruel, greedy, dangerous, armor-scaled, hornèd beasts with curved, knife-sharp talons and sweeping wings. Mister Flitch's book would say that dragons are massively powerful and breathe poisonous flames from sharp-fanged maws.

This dragon isn't like that.

It's about twice the size of a horse.

Its dull, soot-gray, scaly skin sags on its heavy bones. It does have talons, but they are cracked and dull, and its belly scrapes over the rock shards as it drags itself out of its cave. Its wings are folded like tattered umbrellas on its hunched back. Hung on pieces of twine and string and fine chain around its snaky neck are pocket watches, and little clocks, at least twenty of them. As it comes closer, I can hear the watches ticking and bumping against each other. It's a loud, rackety noise.

One of the people in my village is Tansy Thumb the seamstress, who grows blue flowers on vines all over her cottage. She's old and has achy bones in her knees and back that make her walk stiffly and hunched over, especially when the weather is cold and wet. The dragon drags itself along like that—as if its bones hurt.

It pauses and with a cracked talon tip it turns over a lump of rock, inspecting it.

"It hoards watches," Maud whispers. "As you can plainly see."

I nod. And then I realize, with a sudden cold chill, that the white stones and sticks that are scattered about Maud's post aren't stones and sticks, they are human skulls and bleached-white bones.

Maaaah, maaaah, maaah, Poppy complains, fleeing for the path leading down from the slicken heap. Poppy is a smart goat. She knows when trouble is coming.

Then the dragon looks up with eyes that seethe with shadows and sees me, and I know that even though it is old and decrepit, it is still very, very dangerous.

CHAPTER 12

With a sudden heave, the dragon rears up, looming against the darkening sky. A creaky roar erupts from its mouth. The sound echoes, and the coming storm answers with a loud grumble of thunder.

"Eep!" Maud gasps, and starts struggling against the last of the rope that binds her to the post.

"Run if you can," I tell her, and, gripping the knife, I step in front of Maud and the post. At the same moment the dragon launches itself into the air. Its rickety, raggedy wings batter the air as it cranks higher. With a *whoosh*, it banks and swoops toward me and I have to fling myself onto the ground. It zooms past, right over my head. The wind and clatter of its passing roars in my ears, and I climb to my feet and whirl to face it.

At the post, Maud is pulling frantically against the ropes.

Hovering, the dragon fixes her with a fire-red eye.

"Over here," I shout, to distract it.

As its wings continue thunderously thrashing, it wrenches itself around and draws its head back, takes a gasping breath, and a gob of fire blasts from its mouth. The ball of flames wobbles through the air and splatters around me, and I throw myself to the ground again, rolling and leaping to my feet.

The dragon takes another breath as if it's about to blast me with fire again, but it only coughs out a few sparks that fall around me like shooting stars that hiss when they hit the damp ground. Its wings falter and it lurches sideways until it slams into the earth, scrabbling onto its clawed feet and snapping its head around to face me.

It's managed to put itself between me and Maud, who is still tied to the post.

"Leave her alone!" I shout.

Panting, the dragon folds its tattered wings. Its eyes, as big as my hand, are dark, deep with shadows. A leathery membrane—an eyelid—slides across one eye and back— a blink. Slowly, almost painfully, it pulls itself closer to me, its belly grating over the slickens.

I stand ready, gripping my knife.

"Are you all right?" Maud calls from the post. "Did you get burned?"

"The flame passed right over my head," I lie. "I'm not even singed. Can you run?"

"No, curse it!" she shouts back. "This stupid, vile, *ghastly* rope won't break."

The dragon turns its head to look at Maud, then it swivels back to inspect me, leaning close.

"I don't want to fight you," I tell it.

HmmmMMMMmmm, the dragon hums. Its burning hot breath gusts over me. I cough, but the heat of it doesn't bother me.

Slowly, keeping the knife ready, I edge around it, toward Maud and the post. It turns, following me. Its heavy, scaly head is cocked back on its long neck like a snake ready to strike.

Maud is gazing at the dragon with wide eyes, but she seems more fascinated than frightened.

At the post, I raise the knife to cut the last of the rope, and the dragon lurches into an attack, using its big head to shove me away from her. As I hit the ground, the knife flies out of my hand. Maud shrieks as the dragon drags itself closer, and before I can scramble away, it pins me down with a sharply taloned claw on my chest. I struggle against the heavy, hot weight of it, and it leans until my bones creak and I go still, like a mouse under a cat's paw, trying to get enough air into my squished lungs. Gasping for breath, I gaze up into its deep eyes. I search for *evil malicious creature* in there, but I don't see it. Instead, I see . . . sorrow. And age and weariness. The dragon is old, so old. It's been alone for a long, long time.

Time. *That* is what it hoards. The sound of its pocket watches is loud; they hang from its neck, swaying over me, ticking and clinking, gold and silver with shiny glass faces, almost near enough to touch.

Then it turns its head to look at Maud.

Almost as if it's checking to be sure she's all right.

Ohhhh. The *knife*. The dragon thought I was going to use the knife to hurt her. It was protecting her.

The claw is so heavy; I try to get a breath so I can speak. "Dragon," I gasp. "I wasn't going to hurt her."

At that, the dragon pulls back. Then its head comes closer again, and it studies me with its deep eyes. I hold still as its breath washes over me, hot and stale and smelling like burned-out embers.

"I was trying to cut the rope so she can get away," I manage to get out.

"There's no point in talking to it," Maud calls. "It won't talk back to you."

When the dragon speaks, its voice is deep and dry and crackly, and it leans close, peering at me with one huge eye. *What manner of creature is it?*

"Oh!" Maud puts in from the post. "It spoke! What do you suppose it said?"

"You heard what it said," I mutter, without taking my eyes off the dragon that is staring down at me. Shards of rock are digging into my back, but I keep as still as I can.

"Yes, but I didn't *understand*," she says. A gasp. "Oh my goodness. Did you understand it?"

I nod slowly.

At the post Maud makes an excited sound, like *eep!*

Trying to be polite, I say to the dragon, "Could you please let me up?"

The dragon studies me for another moment, and then it lifts its heavy claw from my chest. Quickly I climb to my feet. Holding up my hands to show that they're empty, I edge toward Maud. "Dragon," I say to it. "Maud is still tied to the post, as you can see. She doesn't want you to eat her, like you ate the other propitiations."

The dragon settles itself, nestling its scaly belly into the shards of coal. It makes a sound that is part sigh and part moan, and a trickle of dirty smoke drifts up from its nostrils. With a claw tip it hooks a bleached skull and holds it up. *The human persons whose bones these are were tied to the stake and to them poison was given.* The dragon doesn't frown, like a person would, but somehow I can tell that it is angry. *This was done to poison the dragon. But this dragon eats not such small, soft things and so it eats not the poison. And then it is as you see, youngling.* The dragon tosses aside the skull, which goes rattling away over the coal shards. *They die and turn to bones.* Its gaze slides to Maud. *Yet this small human one dies not.*

"Is it talking about me?" Maud whispers eagerly. "What's it saying?"

I blink. "It's, um, noticing that you're not dead." I glance back at her. "Did somebody try to poison you?"

Her hazel eyes widen. "No!"

"I think you're supposed to be dead. They've poisoned the other propitiations to try to poison the dragon once it eats them. Except it doesn't."

"Doesn't what?" Maud asks.

"Eat them."

Maud makes a scoffing sound. "Well, of *course* it doesn't."

I turn to the dragon. "Is it all right if I get the knife and cut the rest of the rope?"

The dragon gives a long, ponderous sigh. Maud lets out a little squeak as the hot wind gusts past us.

Taking the sigh as a yes, I fetch the knife and, watched carefully by the dragon, I cut through the rest of the ropes, freeing Maud.

Rubbing her arms, she stares up at the dragon, her eyes bright. "Ask it—ask about the watches it hoards. Ask it why it lives here. Ask it why it burns the coal mineworks." She catches her breath. "Oh, and ask it how old it is. I have a theory—"

"Wait," I interrupt. The dragon has started crawling wearily toward its cave. My feet slipping on the coal slickens, I follow; Maud waits behind. "Dragon?" I pant, skidding up to its side, "I'm searching for dragons." My voice shakes, and I steady it. "My village had a dragon once, but it's been gone for a long time."

At the word *time* it stops and cranes its head around to stare at me.

"A long time," I repeat. "Can you tell me . . ." I'm not sure what to ask. "Was the Dragonfell dragon dangerous?"

The dragon is breathing heavily, pants of sparks and clotted smoke. I wonder suddenly if it is sick, maybe even dying. *Dangerous*, it wheezes, and it almost sounds scornful. *All dragons are dangerous, foolish youngling.*

"I mean, was it dangerous to *us*? To its village?"

At that the dragon pauses and turns its head to look at me once more.

"Or did it protect us?" I ask.

For a long moment I gaze up at it. I thought the first dragon I met would be huge and glorious and strong. But this dragon is nothing like what I expected. It's powerful in a different way. It makes me realize that I was stupid to think of dragons as being *evil* or *good*. Those are human words. Dragons are not good or evil, they're just *dragon*.

And I realize something else.

"For a long time," I say, working it out, "the dragons have been disappearing."

The dragon is watching me closely. Its watches are watching me, too. It reaches up with a talon tip and touches them, making them rattle together. The sound of their ticking surrounds us.

"The world is changing," I go on. "That's what Old Shar told me. She said there's no room in it anymore for dragons." I shake my head. It's a sad, hollow thing, to think of a world without any dragons in it. "Your time has passed."

Time, the dragon repeats.

I meet its eyes, and it does something—it shifts, and the ticking of its watches grows louder, and just for a second, the space between one tick and the next, the heavy weight of the time that the dragon carries lifts, and I can see the dragon, not as it is now, all gray and weary, but as it *was*. Proud. Tall. Gleaming silver, not gray, with powerful muscles shifting under its armored skin. A spiky crest, and a broad sweep of wings, and eyes like night and fire. And deep, deep within, it has a spark burning brighter than any sun, any star.

Tick, and time catches up with it, and the dragon is hunched and withered again.

But now I know. I *know*.

Even this old, tired dragon has a spark in it. A flame.

Just like I have a spark in me.

I am dragon-touched. And now I know why.

CHAPTER 13

When I was a tiny kid, I escaped from my crib, toddled out the cottage door, and climbed through the snow to the highest fell.

It was a really strange thing to have done.

Maybe I was chosen from the time I was born, and then I was called, and when I got to the highest fell the dragon gave me a tiny piece of its spark.

Or maybe . . .

Maybe even back then I was interested in dragons, and I went out into the snow, and up to the fell, and was half frozen, and the dragon gave me a bit of its spark to save me. To protect me, because that's what dragons do.

Or maybe both things happened: the dragon called me, and then it saved me.

Either way . . .

What I feel suddenly is a huge wave of relief. There is a *reason* why I'm so strange and different. Why I can't be burned, why I can see in the dark, all of it. If the dragon really did call me, this is why. It's all *for* something.

The dragon has turned to look out over the wasteland toward the town of Coaldowns, which is a smudge of shadow and smoke under a sky heavy with clouds.

"I'm supposed to . . . to save you," I say, feeling like a *foolish youngling* even as I'm saying it. Me, a . . . What did the dragon call humans before? A *small, soft thing*. Me, a kid, and I'm supposed to save the dragons. "I can do that. Or try to do it." Then I realize that I don't even know where to start. "What should I do?" I ask it. "Where should I go? Should I keep trying to find the rest of the dragons? If I can save the dragons, will one of them help save my village?"

The dragon sighs wearily, and a stream of dry-as-dust smoke puffs from its nostrils. *The youngling will find the answers to its questions in Skarth.*

"Skarth?" I repeat.

The city. The cliffs. Skarth. Go there.

"All right," I agree. "Will you come with me?"

No, youngling, it pants. *No. This dragon's lair is here.*

Then slowly, painfully, its belly grating over the sharp rocks, it drags itself into its cave.

Maud and I get about halfway down the dragon's slicken heap when Maud trips on a chunk of rock and goes sprawling. "I'm all right," she says.

Quickly I go to her side and help her to her feet, still half expecting her to flinch away from me. But she doesn't.

Standing, Maud looks down at her palms, which are scraped and bloody. At the same moment, the clouds overhead decide they've been holding on to their burden long enough. Icy rain pours down around us; drops of blood mixed with rainwater and coal dust drip from her hands. "Drat," she mutters, and wipes them off on her coat. "All right. Here's what we'll have to do." She takes a deep breath, as if she's steadying herself. "I left my bags and things at an inn outside of the Coaldowns. We'll have a nice dinner and talk there." She brightens. "I have *so* many questions for you."

Oh, I'll bet she does.

When we get to the bottom of the dragon's slicken heap, Poppy is nowhere in sight. Worry about my goat gnaws at me, but I can't linger here to search for her. We set off on a path that winds through the slickens and mullock heaps. Thunder grumbles overhead and the rain is a heavy, drenching curtain. The sun is close to setting, and the whole world looks gray and black and dismally wet.

Maud hunches into her bulky coat. As we walk, she glances aside at me. "Aren't you cold?"

My first thought is to shake my head no, and tell her that cold doesn't bother me. But instead, I lie. "Freezing," I say, wrapping my arms around myself and hunching the way she is, as if I'm shivering.

Suddenly Maud stops short. Her eyes are wide. "Wait!" she exclaims. "This is terrible."

My heart gives a lurch. It doesn't matter that I lied—she's realized about me being strange and different anyway. She's going to say she doesn't want me to go along with her to the inn after all.

She turns to face me. Her teeth are chattering, and her face is wet with rain. "You've been so nice, and I entirely forgot to ask your name."

"Oh." I feel a wave of relief. "My name's Rafi, son of Jos the Weaver By-the-Water."

She beams. "Rafi Bywater. It's a lovely name."

We keep walking, making a wide circle around the town. I check over my shoulder, looking for Poppy, but there's no sign of her. Eventually we come out onto a soggy path through short, brown grass. To our right, in the distance, is the town, a black and sooty lump in the twilight; to our left, the land flattens into what looks like a boggy wasteland. After trudging for long enough that my stomach is grumbling about missing lunch and is starting to get annoyed about dinner, too, we get to an empty, muddy road. At its edge, Maud stops.

She's gray with tiredness, and her hazel eyes are shadowed. She'd been tied to that post on the mullock heap since yesterday, I realize, and despite her cheerfulness she must have been afraid at the same time, and now all of her strength has run out. "We go left here," she says wearily. "The inn's down this road a mile or two." We turn onto the road. I can't see anything in the distance except more rutted road with the bog on each side of it. "I don't know why they built the inn so far from Coaldowns," Maud goes on. "Maybe because the air is so bad there from the mineworks. You'd think they'd have built the whole town farther away from the mines, really." She chatters on as we walk, as if it's the talking that is keeping her moving. Finally she looks ahead. "Oh! Here we are at last."

On one side of a wide, puddled courtyard is a big building that looks like a stable; next to it, set well back from the road, is a low, stone building with a row of windows along the front. The windows are brightly lit; people hurry through the rain from the stable to the inn's front door. When it opens, I catch a glimpse of a big, crowded room. Scraps of laughter and talking leak out. I smile, thinking of a hot dinner in a merry, warm room.

A room full of people.

"Well, let's go in," Maud says with weary cheerful-ness. "I can't wait to get warmed up. I have extra dry clothes and shoes, too, and I think they'll fit you." She starts toward the inn.

I don't move.

She turns and looks back at me. "Come on, Rafi," she says.

I shake my head. "I can't go into places like this."

She frowns, glances at the inn, then back at me. "Don't be silly. It's an inn. They see all sorts here. It'll be all right."

I hesitate. It's also possible that Stubb and Gringolet have spread the news about the *dragon-touched boy* who they're hunting for Mister Flitch.

"They do a marvelous l-leveret pie," Maud says, shiv-ering. Her eyes have grown wide and water drips from the ends of her curly black hair, and I can see how much she needs to get in out of the rain and cold.

"All right," I agree after another moment. I can try not to be too noticeable.

"Have you ever had leveret pie?" Maud asks as we cross the puddled courtyard.

"I don't even know what a leveret is," I tell her. My stomach growls. We step onto a covered porch and then inside. Maud closes the door behind us.

The low-ceilinged room is warm and crowded and

smells of wet wool and sweat and of hot dinners. Men and women and a few children sit elbow to elbow at round tables. A bright fire burns in a hearth; coats and cloaks are spread on nearby chairs, steaming as they dry. The room is loud with talking and laughter. The floor under my bare feet is sticky, as if something was spilled on it and not cleaned up. I look carefully and see no sign of Stubb and Gringolet.

"Be right with you, miss!" says a gray-haired woman, bustling past with a tray full of steaming bowls.

Maud grins at me. "A leveret is a young rabbit, Rafi. They do it up in a pie with carrots and a lovely gravy." She takes off her wet coat. "I think we should change first, then eat." She eyes my bare feet. "Really, you must be freezing."

"Right, then," the woman interrupts, bustling back, holding the empty tray under her arm, wiping her hands on her apron. She smiles at Maud. "We worried about you last night, miss, thinking you weren't coming back for your things."

"That was very kind of you," Maud answers brightly. "But there's nothing to worry about. I got a little distracted by something, that's all. I think we'll go up to my room and change and then we'll want dinner."

"And hot tea, I expect, on such a foul night," the woman says. Her eyes move to me. The smile drops off her face. "And who might this be?"

"This is Rafi Bywater," Maud says. "Is there any of that delicious pie left from the other night?"

"No-o-o," the woman says, still staring at me. Slowly she looks me up and down, head to foot. "No, I don't think so. Alva," the woman calls over her shoulder. She raises a hand to keep us standing where we are.

From across the crowded room, a woman's deep voice answers, "What is it, Lil?"

The talking and laughing have quieted; people are turning to look at us.

A big woman with muscled arms comes to stand next to the innkeeper, who asks, "What do you make of that one?" She points at me.

I know what she's thinking. *Different means dangerous.*

Alva's eyes narrow as she examines me. "Looks like trouble, Lil."

"Well then, you can stay, miss, as before," the innkeeper says to Maud. "But he can't come in here."

Maud blinks. "What? Whyever not?"

"It's all right," I say to her in a low voice. "You go up and change and have dinner. I'll go outside."

"No, it's not all right," Maud says loudly. "You'll freeze to death out there. It's completely unfair." She turns to the innkeepers. "I've paid for my room, and I've plenty of money for dinner, too."

"Put him out, Alva." Lil jerks her chin at the door.

The big woman reaches over and grabs my arm; she opens the door and shoves me out. "Be off with you," she orders. "And stay out of the stable, too." From inside I hear Maud's high voice shouting and other angry voices, and then the door slams shut.

Night has fallen. The courtyard is empty. I stumble off the porch and the rain pounds on the top of my head, streaming down my face. The bright, happy windows of the inn stare at me. For a minute I just stand there. The little flame inside of me dies down until it's the tiniest spark.

Slowly I trudge away from the inn. At least I know that I am this way—different—for a reason. *That's something*, I tell myself. I've reached the edge of the road when the inn door opens, and then slams closed. I hear footsteps splashing across the courtyard and turn to see Maud, wearing her bulky wet coat again, a heavy leather bag slung over each shoulder.

"What horrible, horrible people," she says, and shoves one of the bags at me.

I take it and stand there staring at her.

"Really!" she says, and she's practically vibrating with fury. "I wouldn't *want* to stay at such a place, not after such a display. How dare they!"

Her anger gets her a mile down the road, back toward Coaldowns, but then she stumbles on a rut in the road, and I catch her arm before she lands in a puddle.

"Drat," she mutters, and stands with her shoulders hunched. "What a mess."

"It's all right," I say. Gently I take the other bag from her and put it over my shoulder. "We have to keep going."

"Yes, I know," she says. She shivers. "Rafi, you are the nicest person I've ever met in my entire life."

I blink. Her cheeks are flushed, and she's shaking with cold. "I think maybe you have a fever," I tell her.

I lead us on through the night. When we get closer to Coaldowns I find a path leading off the main road—we can't go into the town, we'd just end up as propitiations again, and this time maybe they'd poison us first. I blink raindrops out of my eyes and peer ahead. The path leads away from the flat bogland and winds into steep, rocky hills. "This way," I tell her, and we start climbing. When Maud stumbles again, I take her hand and lead her on.

She's definitely feverish, and too tired to go any farther. I brush wet rat-tails of hair out of my eyes and peer through the rain. A bit higher up the hill, across the slope from us, is a dark shape, blurred by the heavy mist.

Shelter, maybe. "Just a little longer," I tell her.

When we get to it, I find that the dark shape is an old sheep shed with three walls made of piled stone and a soggy thatched roof that is half fallen in. A corner of it is out of the rain and wind. Maud has gone silent. I prop her against one wall and pull a bundle of wet straw away from that corner, and make a dry nest with the moldy straw that remains. "Come on," I tell Maud, and lead her inside. I take off her wet coat, help her sit in the straw, and cover her up again with the coat. I crouch before her and rest the back of my hand against her forehead. Yes, she's hot with fever.

"Aren't you c–c–cold?" she asks, gripping the collar of the coat and shivering.

I nod, another lie, and give a pretend shiver. "And hungry," I add. "And worried about my goat."

"Oh, your poor goat, out in this wretched weather," she says sadly.

For a moment I watch her, huddled under the damp coat, shuddering with cold. I've spent all my life looking after my da, so I know how to take care of her. I check in my sack, but all I've got is a rind of cheese, Old Shar's book, my knife, and my tin cup. Until the rain lets up, there's nothing else I can do for her.

No, wait. I still have a spark inside me, and it always

keeps me warm. It can keep her warm, too. Pushing aside the hay, I settle next to Maud and pull the coat over us both. My warmth spreads and I feel her give a last shiver and then go still. She sighs and her head drops onto my shoulder as she falls asleep.

CHAPTER 14

Later, a *maaaaah* wakes me up. It's the middle of the night. Maud is still asleep beside me in the hay. Poppy stands at the edge of our shelter. Seeing her, my heart lifts. Beside her is another goat, one that's taller and bonier and not as furry, with long lop-ears. A thing about goats is that they never want to be the only goat. They want to be part of a herd, and to a goat, even just two goats counts as a herd.

I climb out from under the coat, making sure it's tucked well around Maud, and step outside the shelter. The rain has stopped and the clouds have pulled away, but the stars are hidden behind a pall of sooty smoke that rises up from the Coaldowns in the distance.

I wonder if the time dragon is all right, and if the townspeople came looking for Maud, and what they did when they didn't find her at the stake. Maybe they think the dragon ate her.

I crouch to inspect Poppy. *Maaah, maaaah*, she says, half glad to see me, half eager to be milked. The other goat pokes his nose in, curious. "Hello," I whisper, and reach out to touch one of his soft ears. "Where did you come from?"

Maaaah, Poppy insists.

"All right," I whisper, and I go back into the shed and dig in the sack for the tin cup. After squeezing out a cup of Poppy's warm, sweet milk, I drink it, and then I get another one and carry it carefully into the shelter.

Setting the cup on the ground, I shake Maud's shoulder to wake her.

"Who's that?" she asks in a muzzy voice, blinking in the darkness.

"It's me, Rafi," I say.

She turns her head toward my voice. "Do I know somebody named Rafi?" she asks.

"Yes, you do," I tell her. "Here's some milk." Taking her hand, I help her hold the cup, and then guide it to her mouth. "Mmm," she says sleepily. She drinks half the milk and I catch the cup as it starts to fall from her hands. In a moment she's asleep again. I finish the milk and climb under the coat again and sleep until morning.

When I wake up, Maud is sitting against the wall of the shelter, reading and gnawing on a bit of cheese from my sack. "Good morning," she says cheerfully, and sets aside her book. No, *my* book. Or Old Shar's book, the one about dragons that Mister Flitch gave her.

I sit up and brush the hay out of my hair. "Mornin'," I say.

She grins. "You're Rafi, of course. I do remember. And I'm feeling much better." The goats appear at the shelter opening. Seeing them, Maud's eyes widen. "Oh, there are *two* goats."

I nod and point. "The little one is Poppy. The other one showed up last night."

"She's so elegant," Maud says. "What is her name?"

"He's a he," I say.

"*His* name." Maud laughs. "Elegance. What do you think?"

"It's a good name," I say. Elegance is a male goat and Poppy is a female. They are different breeds, but I wonder if they can make baby goats together. If they did, I'd have an even bigger herd.

I milk Poppy and take the rest of the cheese, and Maud chatters about the shelter, and the goats, and then she picks up the dragon book and shakes it at me.

"I have dire suspicions about this book," she says, drawing her face into a scowl.

I freeze with the cup of milk halfway to my mouth. "You do?"

"Yes. I mean, what sort of title is this?" She glances at the cover and reads the title aloud:

A Guide to the Dragons of the World
Being a History and Study
of the Appearance, Behavior, and Purpose
of the Draconic Species
by
Professor Igneous Ratch
of
The College of Natural Philosophy and Technicrasty,
Skarth

"Have you read it?" she asks. Before I can tell her that I can't read, she goes on. "I've read every book I could find about dragons, but I've never seen this one before. Wherever did you get it?"

"A mill owner named Mister Flitch gave it to a friend of mine," I tell her.

She blinks quickly a few times. "Flitch. Really. How interesting."

"You know him?" I ask.

"No, of course not," she answers. "And now that I've seen a real dragon I rather think that the author, this Ratch person, doesn't know the first thing about dragons."

I set down my cup. "But you do?"

"I do indeed. You saw the Coaldowns dragon, too," she says, and raises her eyebrows. "It's nothing at all like his descriptions." She flips to the back of the book, looks at a page, and finds her place again. "Or hers, maybe. Is *Igneous* a girl's name? Anyway, listen to this." And she reads aloud:

> In these modern times, unlike the days of old, **dragons** have become a rare species; yet they are not quite extinct, having retreated from the usual haunts, lairs, and dens where they once lived, and are now to be found only in such places rarely, and as such have become more like **vermin** and a **plague** upon human persons than the noble creatures they once were, living as they do now in the desolate and abandoned places of the lands.
>
> For the dragons have fallen into ignominy, having become huge, destructive, sly, thievering, greedy, foul, unnatural, selfish, contemptible, parasitical, and entirely treacherous **beasts**.

"The Coaldowns dragon wasn't any of those things," she goes on. "It was wonderful!"

"It was," I agree.

"And the writing style is simply horrible." She reads to herself for a moment, then snorts. "*Xanthodontous?* Hah." She reads some more. "*Furfuraceous or pediculous.* Oh *really*, Professor Ratch?" She flips through the pages. "I think he's pretending he knows what he's talking about, when he's really just making it all up."

I can't think of anything to say. As far as I knew, everything inside a book had to be true; I'd never thought of questioning it before. But Maud has that kind of brain, one that sees past the surface to the truth underneath.

"My own book will be much more accurate," she tells me.

"You're writing a book?" I ask. "About dragons?"

She scrunches up her face. "*Did* I mention that I'm a scientist, Rafi?" She nods. "I believe I did. That's what scientists *do*. I am learning as much as I can about dragons, and writing it all down . . ." Rummaging in one of her bags, she pulls out a little book covered in red leather. "This is my notebook. Once I've figured out what dragons are for, and where they've all gone, and why they left in the first place, I will publish a book."

While we finish our cheese-rind breakfast and she reads aloud what she calls some *particularly egregious passages* from the Ratch book, the clouds move in again and sleet begins to fall outside our shelter.

The coat is spread over the hay, drying, and the goats

are bedded down in the other corner. Maud puts down the book and goes to the edge of the shelter to look out at the view of the Coaldowns. "I think I'd rather wait until the sleet stops before moving on."

"Good idea," I say. Goats hate being wet anyway, so we're better staying here for now.

And . . . we haven't talked about it yet, but she really is a scientist, and she's curious about dragons in the same way that I am, so I'm hoping she'll come with me to Skarth, which is where the time dragon told me to go. But there's something I have to get out of the way first, especially after what happened at the inn.

I clear my throat. "Maud, what do you see when you look at me?"

She turns and shrugs. "A friend."

For a moment I hold that word to me—*friend*—because it's one I haven't heard in a long time. "No, I mean my face."

Being Maud, she takes the question seriously and puts her brain to work on it. She crouches in front of me. "No, don't look away, Rafi," she says. "I'm not afraid of you." She studies me carefully, leaning closer to peer into my eyes. I glare back at her, daring her to say anything.

"Stop that," she orders. Then she reaches out to touch a lock of my hair and rub it between her fingers. "Hmm." She sits back. "I suppose what you're asking," she says slowly, "is why people know from the first moment they see you that you're different from them. That's what happens, isn't it? Like at the inn last night?"

"Yep," I say. "That's it."

"It's partly the hair," she says. "I've seen people before with some red in their hair, but yours is not that color red. It's more like embers. When I first saw you up on the time dragon's heap, you had the light behind you, and it seemed like your hair was on fire." She gives me one of her grins. "Fiery hair alone would be enough to frighten some people." She studies me again. "Then there's your face." I hold myself still while she brushes her fingertips along my cheekbones and then taps my nose and my chin. "Your face is sharp. Nice-looking, I think," she adds quickly, "but not quite like anyone else. Fierce." She gives a half shrug. "It doesn't help that you look so serious all the time. You could try smiling now and then, you know."

"Hah," I say, without smiling.

"Would you care to explain that comment?" she asks.

"No," I tell her. If she comes with me, she'll find out what happens when I smile at people.

"Then there's the way you move." She jumps to her feet and takes a few light, quick steps. "Like that." Then she shakes her head. "No, that's not it. Even when you're just walking around, it seems like you could fly away at any moment." Then she goes on. "Now for the most obvious thing, which is your eyes. It's not just that the centers are dark. Your eyes . . ." She shrugs. "I don't know if I can describe it. The dark of your eyes isn't just brown or black, it's *shadow*. It's almost like it draws the light in." She leans closer, and her voice gets softer. I stay very still. I can feel the warmth of her breath on my face. "I didn't notice before." She moves, peering into my eyes from the side, then from a little farther away. "There's something there, Rafi. Way deep in there. A spark."

I blink, and it breaks the spell. "I know."

"What is it?" she asks.

I think carefully about my answer before I give it. Maud is a *scientist*. She's obsessed with dragons. If she knows that I have the spark of a dragon inside me, she won't think of me as a friend anymore. No, I'll be something scientific to be studied—a specimen.

"Well?" she prompts. "The spark?"

I tell her a lie. "I don't know what it is."

"I don't know either," she says, and then she gives an exaggerated frown. "I don't like not knowing!" A flash, and she's grinning again. "I think most people wouldn't stop to categorize all these things, Rafi—eyes, hair, bones, face, and all that. It just adds up to *wrong* and *different*."

"And people don't like different," I say.

"No," Maud agrees with a sigh, and I realize that she's different, too, and it's turned her into a wanderer—like me.

"Would you come with me to find the dragons?" I ask.

Her smile is blindingly bright. "Rafi, you didn't even have to ask. Of course I am coming."

CHAPTER 15

It is good to have a friend, but the first thing we do is argue about what to do next. "We have to go to Skarth," I tell Maud.

She is rummaging through one of her bags. "Rafi, there are no dragons in Skarth. It's a city. Remember what the Igneous Ratch book says about dragons?" And she quotes it from memory: "They have their lairs *in the desolate and abandoned places of the lands.* We need to do the opposite of go to Skarth—we should go north, where the land is actually, you know, *desolate*? And *abandoned*?"

"But you said you had *dire suspicions* about that book," I protest. "Now you think it's telling the truth about where we can find the dragons?"

She pulls a shirt out of her bag, looks it over, and

tosses it aside. "Skarth is too far out of our way."

"Maud, Skarth *is* our way," I argue. "It's exactly where we have to go. The dragon said so."

She freezes. "The Coaldowns dragon said so?"

"Certain sure it did," I say.

"Oh," she says in a small voice. "What did it say exactly?"

"I asked it questions about dragons," I tell her. "The same questions you have. It said I would find the answers in Skarth."

She wrinkles her nose. "Well then." She heaves a big sigh. "I suppose we do have to go to Skarth." Then one of her quick smiles flashes out. She's like the weather on top of the Dragonfell. Covered with clouds one moment, bright and shiny the next. "But we're not going a step farther until you look presentable, instead of all ragged, as you are now," she says, looking me up and down. "Your clothes are *burned*, Rafi, and awfully holey. It doesn't help, you know."

"You're right," I admit.

"Of course I am." She digs in her bag for a moment, then pulls out a cap. "You can have this!" She plops it onto her own curly black hair. "Also, this." She holds up the shirt she took out before. "And these." She pulls out a pair of pants and a jacket. "Oh, and shoes." She takes those out of the bag, too.

"Why do you have all this stuff?" I ask. All of her clothes are too large for her, I notice, though well made, and the cloth is very fine.

"When traveling, I am always prepared for any eventuality," she says primly.

"Or you stole it from somebody's clothesline," I tease, because I know she didn't.

"Rafi!" She takes the hat from her head and throws it at me.

I duck and the cap flies past me and lands on the new goat's head. While Maud laughs, I climb over the moldy straw and take the cap off of Elegance's horns before he starts to eat it, and put it onto my own head, pulling it down to cover as much of my ember-red hair as I can.

The clothes fit me well enough, even the shoes. I make sure to take the shard of teacup with the blue-painted flower on it, which I found on the Dragonfell, and put it into the pocket of my new pants. Then we pack our things, sling our bags over our shoulders, make sure the goats are ready, and set off. The sun is bright and the air is brisk and washed clean by all the rain, and we put dark, sooty Coaldowns at our backs and head east. Toward Skarth.

We're both hungry for more than a cup of goat milk, so when we get to the inn—the same inn that tossed me out the night before—we stop. At first Maud doesn't want to see those *horrible, horrible people* again, but I tell her that I'm too hungry to care where the food comes from. I wait on the road while she goes in to buy whatever she can get.

After a short while she stalks out of the inn. "I got the food," she snaps, *"and* a lecture about being careful of the dangerous people I might meet on the road. They meant *you* of course. Idiots." She hands me a paper-wrapped package. "Meat pie. Probably delicious." Then she gives one of her sudden grins, like the sun coming out from behind a gray cloud. "On we go!"

As we walk, we talk. Maud has cheerful opinions about everything, from the personal habits of Professor Ratch, who wrote the dragon book, to the way the road is constructed, to what sorts of crops grow best in the soggy soil of the land we're walking through. She's read hundreds of books, and it makes me wonder what she's doing wandering on her own.

"But I'm not on my own," she answers, and pops a bit of dried apple into her mouth. "I'm with you, Rafi."

We're sitting on a stone wall that runs along the edge of the road, watching the goats nibble grass. "Where do you come from?" I ask.

"Oh, you know," she answers, waving a hand. "Around and about. Like you."

I blink. "No, not like me. I'm from a village near the Dragonfell." I get my bearings and point. "It's about three days' walk that way," I tell her. It's funny, but I always know exactly where my village is.

"But now you're a poor, homeless orphan, right?" She makes her face look long and sad.

"No, my da still lives there," I say, surprised. "Are you a homeless orphan?"

"Not exactly," she says, and looks away, blinking. "Tell me about your family."

"Just Da," I say. She doesn't want to talk about herself, that's clear enough. So as we finish our lunch I tell her about my da, and how I never had a mother, and the high, rocky slopes of the Dragonfell, and the village and all the people there—John Smithy and his intricate iron weather vanes, and Tandy Thumb's cottage covered with blue flowers, and Old Shar, and Tam Baker's-Son.

"You must love it very much, your village," Maud says, and she sounds wistful.

I nod. "I do."

There's one thing I don't talk about. Just like she has secrets, so do I. I don't tell her why I had to leave my village, or how Stubb and Gringolet are after me. I don't tell her about how cold and fire don't bother me, or how I can see in the dark. And I don't tell her what I learned from the Coaldowns dragon about who I am and what

I am supposed to do. As far as she knows, I'm like her—I'm just interested in dragons because they're wonderful.

So we have those two big holes in our conversation. We both know they're there. But neither one of us says anything about them.

CHAPTER 16

Maud and the goats and I walk for another day, and the road gets busier with other people walking, or riding horses, or in wagons and carriages drawn by horses or mules. On the next afternoon I hear a low *chug-a-chug-chug* in the distance. At the sound, the people around us start scrambling off the road; a nearby horse snorts and shies away, and its rider speaks soothingly to it and rides it onto the grass. Poppy and Elegance scamper into the nearest field. Then I hear it, a rumbling noise growing louder.

Dragon I think at first—there's smoke and clouds of steam coming up the road behind us—but then it puffs closer, bumping on metal wheels over the ruts in the road. Rattling and snorting loud enough that it makes my ears hurt, it jolts by us, a kind of wagon with a fat-bellied copper tank studded with shiny rivets, rods going up and down, oily gears turning, and a short chimney belching smoke. I catch a glimpse of two women perched on a high seat, one of them holding a hat on her head, the other gripping a metal rod—for steering, I guess—and then they are past. A cloud of dust and smoke swirls in the road and starts to settle.

"What was *that*?" I ask.

Maud coughs and waves the smoke away. "Haven't you ever seen one before?"

I shake my head, staring as the thing rattles off into the distance.

"It's a vaporwagon," Maud tells me. "It's not going to hurt you, you silly goats," she mock-scolds as Poppy and Elegance prance back onto the road.

"What makes it go?" I ask.

"It has a coal-fired, steam-driven engine. The coal burns and boils the water, and the boiling steam makes the engine go." Maud shrugs. "I don't really understand how it works. You don't see vaporwagons out in the country like this very often because the roads are so bad, but there are loads of them in—I mean, in some of the cities."

"A steam-driven engine that runs on coal," I repeat, remembering what Old Shar said about Mister Flitch's factory mills that make cheap cotton cloth. "The factories are steam-driven too, aren't they?"

"Ye-es," Maud answers, blinks a few times, and then starts talking about a yellow flower that is growing next to the road.

As we get closer to Skarth, huge wagons drawn by the biggest horses I've ever seen start to lumber past us, long convoys of them; whatever they're carrying is covered with stained canvas. Empty carts pass, going the other direction.

"Coal," Maud tells me. Skarth is a *center of industry*, she says, which I assume means it's stuffed full of factories that eat up the coal and spit out clouds of black smoke after.

Something is tickling at the edge of my thoughts. The factories in Skarth run on coal, maybe even the coal that's mined in the Coaldowns. Where the time dragon keeps breaking the mineworks. The dragon who said that the answers to my questions were in . . . Skarth. Dragons and factories and coal—they must be connected somehow.

It's late afternoon as Maud and I come to the top of a hill, and we stop to take in the view. Filling the entire valley below us is the city. The sun is leaning toward the distant fells, and a thick haze lies over the land. Sticking up through the haze are hundreds of tall smokestacks like dark fingers pointing at the sky, with black smoke billowing from their tops. A wide river makes a curve before the city; it's silver in the afternoon light, and crowded with barges—more coal—and smaller boats. Other roads lead into the city, where lights in the buildings are beginning to come on. There are more lights, too—fires like giant furnaces, and flames that burn at the tips of some of the smokestacks.

Poppy bumps the back of my leg and complains, *maaaah*, that it's past time for milking.

Maud is staring at the city laid out before us. "Are you sure we have to do this, Rafi?" she asks, with a little tremor in her voice.

"Yes." I take a deep breath. "Do you remember me talking about Mister Flitch?"

Her eyes blink rapidly. "The one who gave your friend the Igneous Ratch book. I remember." She swallows.

"I can't . . ." I'm not sure how much to tell her. "Mister Flitch doesn't like me very much. He—"

"You've *met* him?" Maud interrupts. "I thought . . ." She shakes her head. "Never mind. Go on. Mister Flitch doesn't like you. And?"

"The thing is," I tell her, "Flitch is from here." I point at the city. "He lives in Skarth."

Then her face brightens. "Oh, I *see*. You can't just walk into the city and start looking for . . ." She shrugs.

". . . For whatever it is that the Coaldowns dragon thinks we're going to find here."

"Dragons," I tell her. "We're looking for dragons."

"Yes, of course we're looking for dragons," Maud says impatiently. Then her eyes widen. "Wait a moment. Wait, wait, wait." She grabs my arm. "Rafi. Are you saying there's a dragon *here*, in Skarth?" Then she shakes her head. "There can't be. It's impossible."

"I don't know for certain sure," I admit. "But the Coaldowns dragon told us to come here." And then I add, "It mentioned cliffs."

"Oh!" she exclaims, "I know—" She snaps her mouth closed, blinks twice, and then starts again. "Cliffs," she says more carefully. "We'll have to go into the city and look for cliffs."

I don't say anything, but I'm starting to suspect one of the things that Maud doesn't want to tell me. She lied about being from *around and about*. It seems she knows about Skarth. She might even be from here.

CHAPTER 17

After sunset, the goats crowd close to me as we walk down the hill toward Skarth. The houses get bigger, and closer together, and the rutted dirt road turns into a cobblestoned street. A vaporwagon rattles past, and then another one. The air is heavy with the smell of smoke and loud with a kind of humming roar that isn't any one thing, like voices or factory noises or wagon wheels on the streets, it's all those things at the same time.

"How many people live here?" I ask as we walk down a dark street edged with tall buildings built of bricks. Lights shine from every window. The goats prance along behind us.

Maud shrugs. "Oh, hundreds of thousands, I expect."

I didn't think there were that many people in the

entire world. Never mind in just one city.

We're heading down a narrow street when a ragged boy with a smudged face steps suddenly in front of me, and I bump into him.

"Oi, watch where you're going," he complains.

Maaaah, Poppy puts in.

Another ragged boy bumps me from behind, then gives me a shove. "Move it."

I shove back, and my spark flickers. Maud steps closer. "Rafi," she warns. At the same time, somebody else bumps into her and she stumbles. I catch her with one arm and turn to glare at the two ragged boys again, but they're gone.

"This isn't a very nice part of the city," Maud explains, hoisting her bag onto her shoulder again. "Come on. Let's skulk this way."

I give her a sharp look, thinking she's enjoying this more than she should be.

With a grin and a shrug, she turns a corner, and we go into an even narrower, darker street. The goats follow. "There," Maud points. A dim light is shining from a grimy window with a handwritten sign in it. "Rooms for rent," she says. "It won't be very nice, but we can stay there and get some dinner, and look for the cliffs tomorrow." She heads up a set of stone stairs and into the rooming house. Leaving the goats to nibble on whatever trash they can find, I follow.

Inside is a dark hallway that smells like boiled cabbage and sweaty shirts. A tired-looking woman with stringy brown hair emerges from the dimness. "Want a room?" she asks. Before we can answer, she says, "Pay up front. Six shillings."

"That's fine," Maud says brightly. Setting down her bag, she digs inside. She's had money to pay for everything, so far, silver and gold coins that she keeps in a fat leather purse. "That's odd," she says slowly. "I thought I put it in . . ." She swallows, then goes to her knees and starts pulling everything out of the bag—shirts, her books, a comb, an extra pair of socks. No purse. She looks up at me with wide eyes. "Those boys. The ones who bumped into you. They were pickpockets."

It takes me a second to figure out what she means. We don't have thieves in the Dragonfell. "They stole your purse?" I ask.

She nods and starts stuffing everything back into the bag.

"Can't pay, get out," the woman says, and jerks her chin toward the door.

Maud gets to her feet. "But we—"

"Out," the woman repeats.

"Come on," I say to Maud, and we stumble out of the rooming house and into the dark, smelly street.

Maud looks gray with worry, and she speaks through stiff lips. All of a sudden, this isn't an adventure anymore. "Rafi, I have absolutely no money at all." She stops and takes a shaky breath. "Not even a penny. What are we going to do?"

"I don't know," I tell her. "I've never been in a city before."

"We'll have to find somewhere to sleep." She looks around, as if we'll find a spare bed lying in the street.

"Onward?" I ask.

She gives me a tired smile. "Yes."

As we wander the city, we pass huge brick buildings with rows of windows and fat smokestacks that belch clouds of sooty smoke into the air. The streets are dark, with just a lantern here and there, or a fire in a heap of trash, with ragged figures huddled around it. We pass a warehouse, looming and silent in the night, and another factory, still lit up and rumbling with noise. A bitter wind blows at our backs. We turn down one street, and another, and go along a trash-clotted alley until we come to a square yard enclosed on all four sides by ramshackle six-story houses. The air smells like the swirling cess-pool in the middle of the yard, and of the piles of rotting garbage. Strung across, from one crack-paned window to another, are ropes with ragged laundry hung out to dry. As I watch, a red-eyed rat scurries along one of the clotheslines. A few shadowy people are gathered around a fire.

"I can't walk another step," Maud whispers.

"Neither can I," I say.

Without speaking, we find a space next to a wall and clear away the trash, and we settle on the hard ground. The goats wander into the yard, nosing in the garbage, looking for something to eat. We have no place to sleep but this, and no dinner.

Maud rests her head on her bended knees. "Rafi," she says, and I can hear the tears in her voice. "This is awful."

"It is," I agree. I shift closer to Maud to try to share my warmth with her, but I can feel her shivering.

"Will you tell me something nice, Rafi?" she whispers. "So I don't have to think about how hungry I am?"

I think for a minute. I know what will cheer her up. "Will you tell me why you're so interested in dragons?"

"Oh, well," she says, looking up, and her hazel eyes go dreamy, as if she's seeing something far away from this dark, stinking place. "Because dragons are wonderful. I mean, think about it!" Her face brightens. "Professor Ratch's book says they're dangerous and all that, and I know these days people don't like them very much, but really they must be magnificent creatures. Can you imagine what it would be like to be flying wingtip to wingtip with other dragons, soaring over a city like this one, seeing the tiny streets and the lights and the factories below and then leaving it behind, swooping up above the clouds to fly with stars all around you?"

"Yes, I can imagine it," I say. I've had dreams like that before, full of fire and stars and the swift rush of flight.

"Glorious," she says with a happy sigh.

"There was a dragon on the Dragonfell once," I tell her.

She rolls her eyes. "Of *course* there was, Rafi. The *Dragon*fell? You know, I would have come there eventually, for my research. Maybe we'd have met then. If we hadn't met before, I mean. Do you know anything about your dragon?"

"Not much," I say, not wanting to mention that it burned my da and made me dragon-touched. "People don't talk about it. I do know that it hoarded teacups painted with blue flowers." I take out the shard of teacup from my pocket and hold it out to her.

She peers at it in the dim light. "Oh!" she breathes. "That's lovely." She leans her head against my shoulder. "They all hoard something different, isn't that fascinating? And not like what Ratch says in his stupid book, not jewels or princesses. The Coaldowns dragon hoards pocket watches. I've read about one that hoards sea glass, and one that hoards silver spoons, and one that hoards spiders. Can you imagine? A spider-hoarding dragon?" She falls silent. Then she gives my arm a comforting pat. "You're like me. You *can* imagine."

I can. But . . .

In my coat pocket I can feel the crumpled paper, Gringolet's notice that I don't know how to read.

Maud doesn't know why I left the Dragonfell. She thinks I'm like her—that I want to find the dragons because I'm curious about them. She doesn't know that I've been lying to her since the moment we first met.

CHAPTER 18

I wake up in the dark before morning. Maud is still asleep, with her black coat hunched around her.

Nearby, Poppy's eyes blink open. "Don't come with me," I whisper to her, getting to my feet. Maud will know I'm coming back if the goats are still here.

I slip away, determined to find us something for breakfast before we start our day of searching the city for the cliffs and the Skarth dragon. The streets are narrow, and dark, and twisty, and I can smell bread baking. It reminds me so much of my village and of Tam Baker's-Son, that I feel a little hollow, and not just with hunger.

Following my nose through the dimly lit streets, I round a corner, and run right up against somebody I know.

Gringolet.

She is just as strange and threatening as she was the first time I saw her, talking to my da outside our cottage. She's added a row of pins in her eyebrows, and she looks even thinner and more drawn-out than she did before. "Well, well," she says in her rough voice, drawing a long, glitteringly sharp pin out of her coat sleeve. "I've been scouring the city for you, spark boy, and here you are!"

I look around quickly for Stubb, but he's nowhere to be seen.

"Now, come along nicely," Gringolet says.

I take a step back. "Why would I do that?"

"Because you're running out of time." She points at me with the pin. "If Mister Flitch doesn't get what he needs from you, and soon, he'll take it from your village."

My eyes narrow. Mister Flitch said the same thing to me, back in Old Shar's front yard. "He told me that he'd take something from *under* my village," I say. "But there's nothing under my village except rock."

"Oh *really!*" she sneers. "But what if the rock under your village is . . . coal?"

I stare. That possibility hadn't occurred to me. Mister Flitch's factories run on coal. He wouldn't dig up my village to get the coal under it. Would he?

Of *course* he would.

And if he did, the Dragonfell would end up looking like the Coaldowns—sooty and dirty and surrounded by mullock heaps. And my not-quite-friend Tam would spend his whole days "under," just like the miner boy I'd met there.

I gulp. "Mister Flitch said . . . he said he wanted something from me. What do I have that he wants?"

Gringolet moves snakelike to the side. "You tell me, boy."

The only thing I can think of is . . . "My spark?"

She nods. Her eyes are fixed on me. She never blinks, I realize, and she never looks away.

"But he can't take my spark. Can he?" I ask.

"*Can* he?" she asks, and her voice sounds twisted and bitter.

I blink. Wait. Gringolet is so strange and ashy. Like a fire gone out. Did she used to be different? "Did you have a spark once?" I ask her.

"*Did* I?" she snipes.

"Flitch took it," I guess.

"No, he didn't," she says. She edges closer, still holding the pin, ready to strike. "I gave it to him."

I shake my head, because it doesn't make any sense. "You were dragon-touched, and you gave up your spark?"

"I had my reasons," she says, and there's that bitterness

in her voice again. "You have reasons, too," she goes on. "Unless you *like* being a freak and an outcast. You have a choice to make, just as I did."

A choice? I stare at her, realizing what she means. Flitch wants me to give up my spark to save my village.

Gringolet still has her unblinking eyes fixed on me. Suddenly she glances to the side and gives a little nod, and I whirl around to see Stubb, sneaking up on me from behind.

I dodge, quickly.

"Grab him!" Gringolet shouts, and lunges at me with the pin, and I squirm out of Stubb's reaching hands and sprint away.

"Make your choice!" Gringolet screams after me.

I whirl around a corner and race down another alley, and around another, and then lean against a brick wall, panting. There's no sound of pursuing feet. But they know I'm here in the city—they'll be searching.

I catch my breath. I have to think about this.

Gringolet was like me, dragon-touched, and she gave up her spark. And now she's this ashy, bitter thing. That's what'll happen to me, too, if I give my spark to Mister Flitch.

And what will he do with it, once he has it?

I have no idea.

I shake my head and push off from the wall. Gringolet

says I have a choice to make, but what Mister Flitch is offering is no kind of choice at all.

Keeping an eye out for Gringolet and Stubb, I hurry through the dark alleys, back to where I left Maud. Now I know what he wants from me, but I'm not stupid enough to make any deals with Mister Flitch. My plans won't change. I still have to find the dragons, and help them, and find out what it really means to be dragon-touched. Certain sure I'm not giving up my spark before I find out why, exactly, I have it.

And it's another secret that I'll be keeping from Maud.

When I get back to the dilapidated square where we spent the night, a new goat has joined Poppy and Elegance. She is white, and very fat, with a little goat beard on her chin, and curved black horns.

Maud blinks her eyes open. "Oh," she says in a rusty voice, sitting up. "A new goat."

"Yep," I say, surveying them, my own little herd, and it makes me feel a lot less worried about Gringolet.

"What will you name him?" Maud asks.

"*Her* name is . . . Fluffy," I decide.

"Fluffy," Maud repeats. "Really?"

I nod. It's a good name, even though Fluffy's white fur is limp and dusted with soot.

The sky is turning gray with dawn as Maud gets stiffly

to her feet and we leave the trash-filled square.

"I was thinking," Maud says, giving me a wan smile. "There's a river. That's most likely where we'll find cliffs, don't you think?"

I nod, and we make our way through the awakening city, keeping to the most secret alleyways. The goats follow, stopping now and then to nibble at a bit of trash on the ground, then scampering to catch up.

After an hour of skulking, we get to the river that sweeps in a wide bend around the city, and to the docks, where silent steamships ride at anchor out in the rushing water, and the cranes and pulleys for loading them are just creaking to life. The air smells dank and sour.

We reach the end of the docks and the warehouses. To our right, the river surges past. To our left is a pebbly beach and steep, white cliffs.

"If you were a dragon," Maud muses, studying the cliffs, "where would you lair?"

"High up," I answer, thinking of the Dragonfell.

She cranes her neck. "I don't see anything."

"Neither do I," I say. Not even with my farseeing eyes. "Come on."

Carrying our bags, I lead Maud onto a path that winds along the edge of the river. The cliff to our left glimmers white in the rosy morning light.

"My goodness," Maud says faintly. "I'm hungry."

I don't bother answering. Our footsteps go *crunch, crunch, crunch* over the pebbly riverbank.

And then I see it. A spot of shadow on the cliff face, high overhead. "Look!" I point it out.

Maud squints. "Where?"

I lead her closer and then point again. "There." Way overhead, high on the cliff face, is an opening like a wide, dark mouth.

"I see it," Maud says breathlessly. She peers at the cliff face. "There are handholds. . . ."

Leaving the goats at the base of the cliff, we climb up. When we reach the cave, we crawl in and Maud pulls a candle and matches out of one of the bags.

Lit by the candle's wavery flame, the cave is softly pink and circular, and its floor is sandy. There are dusty, leather-bound books stacked along the curve of the walls, all the way up to the ceiling. More books are scattered on the floor, as if they've fallen from the stacks, and others are lying open, as if somebody's been reading them.

"Oh, Rafi," Maud says, pointing. Her eyes are sparkling with excitement. "There it is!"

In the flickering candlelight I see, curled atop a pile of books almost as tall as I am, a narrow strip of darkness as long as my hand. Its eyes are little points of fire.

The Skarth dragon's scales are shadow dark, its tiny claws are jeweled, and it has no wings.

I step closer. The dragon is perched on an open book. Without paying us any attention, it shifts, turns a page with a sharp claw tip, and settles in again, reading. It's wearing a small pair of spectacles with gold frames.

"Hello," I say to it.

No answer, just a snort that releases a thread of gray smoke that wavers toward the curved cave ceiling.

I try to think of what Da would want me to say to be polite. "I hope you don't mind us coming into your cave uninvited."

No answer.

Maud steps up beside me. "Did it say anything?" she whispers.

"No," I tell her. "Maybe it's busy and doesn't want to be interrupted."

"Perfectly understandable." Maud smiles up at me. "I'm often that way when I'm reading."

The dragon's perch on the open book is at about the same height as my eyes. "Hello again," I say to it. "I'm Rafi, and my friend here is Maud."

The dragon looks up from the page. With a claw, it takes off the spectacles and they fall to dangle from a chain around its scaly neck. Its glowing eyes look me up and down.

What is it? it asks. Its voice is slithery and rough at the same time.

"I'm a boy," I tell it.

Next to me, Maud leans closer, holding the candle, as if she hopes to join the conversation.

Tsa, tsa, spits the dragon, with a glare at her. *Tell it to go away.*

"Maud," I say quietly, "it doesn't want to talk to you right now."

"Oh." She blinks a few times, and I know she's disappointed. "All right." She goes to one of the piles of books and tilts her head; I think she's trying to read the titles written on their spines.

The dragon makes the match-striking sound again. *Tsa!* Its tail lashes. *Keep that flame away from my books.* It stands on its four claws, its whole tiny body quivering, its eyes glowing.

She's pulled a book from the pile; opening it, she starts to read. A bit of melted wax from the candle drips onto the page.

Tsa! exclaims the dragon. It perches at the edge of its book pile, then leaps and slithers through the air toward Maud. She looks up and, seeing it coming, drops the book; the dragon swoops down and snatches it up before it hits the floor, sets it on top of another wobbly pile of books, and then rushes like a shadowy whirlwind toward Maud.

Tsa! Out! it hisses. *Out!*

Maud backs away, still holding the candle. "What's it saying?"

"It wants us to leave," I say, and duck as the dragon loops around the room and darts at Maud again, and this time, snarling, it slashes at her face with its claws, barely missing her.

Maud drops the candle and tumbles to the floor, covering her head with her arms. "Rafi!" she squeaks. "In my pocket! Quickly, before it scratches my eyes out! Propitiation!"

CHAPTER 19

Propitiation?

Oh, right. Dragons like presents to add to their hoards—*that* is what a propitiation is. Ducking as the dragon darts past, I crawl closer to Maud and reach into her coat pocket.

The book is there—the Professor Ratch book. I yank it out and jump to my feet, holding it over my head. "Skarth dragon!" I shout. "We brought this for you."

The dragon is a sliver of darkness; it zips past, and the book is snatched out of my hand. Muttering to itself, it returns to its nest, puts on its spectacles, and opens the Ratch book.

Phew!

A few paces away, Maud peers out from under her

arms. She reaches over and picks up the fallen candle, which is still burning, and sets it upright in the sand. "I hoard books, too," Maud says, giving me a shaky smile, "when I'm at home." She sits up, digs in her other pocket, pulling out her red notebook and pencil. "I just have to write a few things down," she says. "And then we can ask the dragon our questions." She cocks her head. "*You* can ask it our questions, I mean."

While she writes, and the dragon reads, I have another look around. There are hundreds of books in here. Maybe thousands. A short passageway leads to another cave that is completely stuffed with more books. The air is dry and dusty, and I can see why the dragon is so careful about open flames. As I come back into the main cave, the two sparks that are the dragon's eyes watch me. It makes little grumbling noises to itself.

I go and lean against the cave wall near its stack of books. "My name is Rafi," I tell it. "I'm from a village called the Dragonfell. Our dragon has been gone for a long time. It hoarded teacups painted with blue flowers."

The dragon makes a sound like *hmmmph*. It pushes its spectacles higher on its tiny snout and peers down at a page in the Ratch book about dragons.

"Is the propitiation we brought all right?" I ask.

It doesn't answer. I wait. Maud is watching with her pencil poised over her red book, ready to take notes.

Tsa, it complains at last. *This book.* It crouches, curling its tail around itself like a cat. *Has it read this book, Rafi of Dragonfell?*

"Have I read it, you mean?" I shake my head. "No." And even though Maud is listening, I add, "I can't read."

Rafi sees far, the dragon says.

"Yes," I tell it, and I don't say anything more because Maud can hear me.

Tsa, it says, as if disgusted. *Cannot read. Cannot see to read.* With a curved claw it taps the spectacles that are still perched on its snout.

I have no idea what it's talking about.

Tsa. The dragon nestles into the open book. *Was library in Skarth. Big library, many, many lovely books. This one laired there. Then, library closed.*

"Closed?" I ask. "Why?"

A ripple passes down its length—a shrug. *Factories come. No more library. This dragon take book out, bring here.* It raises a claw and gestures at the cave. *Take, bring, take, bring.*

"You stole all of these books from the Skarth library?" I ask. I get a sudden picture in my head of the little streak of shadow that is the dragon flying back and forth between this cave and a big building in the city, carrying books even larger than its whole body in its tiny claws.

Not steal. It glares at me. *Rescue.* It snorts an annoyed puff of smoke from its tiny nostrils. No flame, though. *Library closed*, it says again. *Then, library burn.*

"The library burned down?" I ask. And then I realize what must have happened. "And you were blamed for it, weren't you?"

The dragon doesn't answer. Perched on its book, its tiny face looks ancient and strangely wise.

From the corner of my eye I can see Maud, wide-eyed, scribbling rapidly in her red notebook.

"It's the same in Coaldowns," I say. "They blame the dragon there for burning the mineworks."

And me. I was blamed for a fire I didn't set.

I take a deep breath. "Old Shar—she's a friend from my village—she says there's no room in the world for dragons because things are changing, and an old lady in Barrow told me the same thing. She said that things used to be different, many years ago, and the Coaldowns dragon showed me what dragons used to be like. It was powerful, and beautiful." I shake my head. "But it's not just that things are changing. The dragons are being driven out, aren't they?"

And the dragon-touched, like me, are, too. But I don't say that part of it out loud.

The tiny dragon looks at me for a long moment. *Driven out of lair*, it says. *Then hunted.*

"Hunted," I repeat. "Why?"

As an answer, the tiny dragon flicks the spectacles off its nose and glares at me, its eyes like tiny sparks. Suddenly it leaps to its feet, and with a sharp claw it rips a page out of the Igneous Ratch book. In a flurry and a frenzy, it tears out more pages, shredding them until the air is filled with scraps of paper floating around us.

The dragon perches at the edge of what is left of the book. Opening its tiny maw, it makes a snarly sound and then spits out a sharp needle of fire that darts to one of the scraps of paper, which bursts into flame. One by one it ignites all the scraps, and they burn, turning to ash as they fall to the sandy floor.

"It really, really doesn't like that book, does it?" Maud asks.

"I guess not," I agree.

Ratch book, the dragon says scornfully. *Is lies lies lies more lies.* It glares at the ashes that are all that are left of the book.

"This doesn't exactly answer my question," I point out. "Why are the dragons being hunted?"

Tsa. The dragon settles down again. *Book says dragons are evil.*

I remember what Maud read aloud from the Ratch book. "Ratch said dragons are huge, destructive, greedy, foul . . ." I try to remember the rest of it.

". . . entirely treacherous beasts," Maud finishes for me.

Is lies. Book is lying reason for hunting, say dragons treacherous. Book is treacherous. The Flitch and his ashy one. They hunt dragons. They are thieves. They drive dragons from lair, they burn, they hunt.

The *ashy one* must be Gringolet. "Why?"

Not know human reasons, the dragon answers scornfully.

I'm a human, and *I* don't know the human reasons either.

I turn to explain it all to Maud. "The Skarth dragon just told me that the dragons are not just being driven out, they're being hunted by Flitch." And by Gringolet, but Maud still doesn't know about her, and I'm not telling her now.

"We have to help," Maud says. She looks strangely grim. "We have to stop my—that Mister Flitch, I mean, from hunting any more dragons. Rafi, do you think he's killing them?"

"I don't know," I answer. "He must be." I have a sudden realization. "Maybe that's what happened to the Dragonfell dragon." I turn back to the dragon. "What can we do to help?"

The tiny dragon's tail is twitching, making it look like an annoyed cat. It leans forward. *Is book*, it says.

"A book?" I ask, blinking in surprise.

"What book?" Maud interrupts.

"Shhh," I tell her. "What book?" I ask the dragon.

Is true dragon book. Is maps and list of all dragons and lairs. Is map where to find greatest of all dragons. Glass dragon. Youngling Rafi must find glass dragon. It sees. It knows.

"The book has a map in it," I tell Maud, "of where to find a glass dragon." I ask the Skarth dragon, "Why can't you just come with us?"

Dragon not leave lair.

"Why not?" I ask.

The dragon's tiny face crinkles, making it look even more fierce. *Is LAIR.*

"All right," I tell it. The Coaldowns dragon wouldn't leave its lair, either. It must be a dragon thing. "Then will you give us the book with the map in it?"

Not have. Stolen from library.

"Who stole it?" I ask, even though I've already guessed the answer.

Is Flitch has book. Rafi youngling must steal it back.

CHAPTER 20

Maud and I sit cross-legged on the sandy floor of the dragon's lair and plan what we're going to do.

"You really can't read?" she asks me.

"No," I say. "I'm . . . well, I'm too stupid."

She makes a scoffing sound. "Oh, stop. *You* stupid? You're the cleverest person I know, Rafi!"

I shake my head, but don't argue with her any more about it. I turn to check on the dragon. It is curled on its stack of books like a cat, watching us with its ember eyes. "Can't you just tell us what's in the book?" I ask it.

As an answer, it opens its tiny mouth and emits a soundless snarl.

"Never mind," I say quickly, and turn back to Maud.

"It's not a very nice dragon, is it?" she whispers.

"No," I whisper back. "But I'm not sure *nice* is the right word to use when talking about dragons."

She gives a surprised half laugh, as if she's forgotten how tired and hungry she is. "You're right, of course."

"Anyway," I go on, "the fact that I can't read means we'll both have to search for the book. I wonder where Flitch is hiding it."

"It's not at home," Maud says slowly, ". . . at Flitch's home, I mean. Um." She frowns. "The book must be in his office in his factory. That's the most likely place. Don't you think?"

"Sounds right to me," I tell her. Then I call out, "Skarth dragon, can you show us where Mister Flitch's factory is?"

As an answer, the dragon flits over to a pile of loose papers, paws through them, and pulls one out, which it drops in front of us and then goes back to its books.

Maud inspects the paper. "This is a map. See the river, here?" She points.

I shrug, not bothering to look.

"And here's the factory," she goes on. "We'll have to sneak in at night." Then Maud looks straight at me, her eyes wide, because she's thinking the same thing that I am.

"Tonight," I say.

"I might die of hunger before then," Maud says seriously.

The tiny dragon makes a scoffing sound and launches itself from its pile of books. It zips away, deeper into the cave. A moment later it returns with a paper-wrapped package gripped in its claws, which it drops on the sandy floor between me and Maud. Opening it we find dried fruit, and hard biscuits, and a bottle of water.

We both tear into the food, and then Maud writes some more in her book, and I pace around the cave waiting for night. I can feel my spark burning away inside me. It feels brighter, hotter, as if I might burst into flame. As if I'm getting closer to learning what it really means to be dragon-touched.

After sunset, we climb down the cliff face, from one handhold to the next, until we get to the stony shore of the river. The moon has come up, so it's not entirely dark, and a glow of streetlights comes from the city, not far off.

The goats crowd around, pressing their faces against my legs.

And there's a new goat. He's a big billy with curved horns, thick brown fur, and a long beard that frames his face and straggles from his chin. He's standing by himself on a chunk of rock at the edge of the river watching me and the other goats, but not coming any closer.

"Hello!" I call to him. Even Maud won't mistake this

one—it'll be obvious even to her that he's not a female goat.

In answer, he raises his upper lip and sneers at me. Not friendly.

I decide to call him Gruff.

"That's four goats," I say to Maud, feeling unaccountably happy.

"Ah, your goats," Maud murmurs, and pulls the notebook out of her coat pocket. "Very interesting." Using the moon for light, she writes something down with a pencil, then snaps the book closed. "All right. Let's go."

Feeling slightly sick that I still haven't told her that I can see in the dark, or that Mister Flitch has reasons of his own for sending his hunters after me, I lead her along the river path to the docks. Followed by the goats, we clatter through the alleyways, as Maud leads us toward the factory.

When we get there, the goats go silent. That's the way they are at night, because they are prey, and they know that when it gets dark they have to be small and quiet so somebody—like a wolf—doesn't eat them. The new goat, Gruff, puts himself between the rest of them and the street, and they settle onto the cobblestones of the alley.

Maud and I peer around a corner at the end of the alleyway. Across cobblestones that gleam in the moonlight, the factory is silent and dark, except for a glow in a window near the main door. There's a night watchman on guard.

"I know how we can get in," Maud whispers. I see the flash of her teeth as she grins. "This is fun, isn't it?"

"Not entirely," I say, checking the street. It's empty.

"We'll go around the back," Maud says. "There should be a door to the steam-engine room."

"It's all clear," I whisper. "Let's go."

Stealthily, we slip out of the alley and around to the back of the factory. To Maud it must look dark, but I can see right away where the back door is, a few steps down from street level. I point to it and Maud nods. We have to cross an open area to reach it, so I put my hand on her arm, holding her still while we listen. The city is never quiet—there's always a hum and a distant clatter, a glow of lights and fires, a smell of chimney smoke and sewers. But nobody is near the factory, except us.

Quickly we dart across the road to the back, and down the three steps to the door.

Locked.

"Oh *drat*!" Maud whispers. She leans close and breathes into my ear. "We'll have to go down the coal chute. It should be near here."

I scan the wall of the factory and spot it at once. A hinged metal door about my height.

The door is heavy, and as I open it the hinges make a rusty creaking sound that I'm sure the night watchman is going to hear.

"Climb in, quick!" I tell Maud, holding open the door.

She does, and makes a sound like *meep* as her feet slip out from under her and she tumbles away. A second later I follow her, zooming down a chute that leads from the door to a huge coal pile at the bottom. She's waiting for me there, smudged all over with coal dust, but still smiling. "That was fun," she whispers.

We climb down off the coal heap.

Coal for running the factory; coal, I guess, which came from the Coaldowns. And which can't ever come from my village.

The steam-engine room is cavernous and dark. From the walls hang hooks and chains holding up enormous gears; fat iron pipes cross the ceiling. Filling most of the room is a row of huge, silent engines with pistons and stilled gear-wheels. They're steam engines, like on the vaporwagons, except fifty times bigger, and they run Mister Flitch's millworks. The floor is covered with dust and sharp bits of coal and pieces of metal.

"This way," Maud says, and leads me across the room to a narrow iron staircase that leads to the first floor of the factory. We climb up to a catwalk, and then up another ladder to a big mill room. Here is all silence, too. The floor is ankle deep in fluff.

"Those are . . . those must be the looms, for weaving the cloth," Maud says, pointing to a row of smaller machines. Bobbins of thread are lined up in the spinneries, and the belts that turn their motors are still. They're nothing at all like my da's wooden loom, which says only *swath* and *whirr* and *thump-thump*. It makes me miss my da with a fierce ache.

Then Maud grabs my coat sleeve. "Guard!" she whispers.

Silently we crouch and edge into one of the aisles between the metal loom frames. I hear an echoing *clunk-clunk-clunk*, and a watchman comes up the iron staircase from the catwalk. He holds up a lantern. Its beam of light shines over the mill machines. Maud and I hold our breaths. I can practically hear my heart beating, and I'm half afraid it's going to give us away.

Then we hear his footsteps leaving, and the light recedes, too.

"Phew!" Maud whispers.

"Where to now?" I ask.

"The offices are upstairs," Maud says. "I mean, they probably are."

We make our way from the main mill room, through some other storage rooms, all dark and silent, to a door that opens to a staircase leading up.

"Wait," Maud whispers. She points. "Let's see what's behind that door."

I follow as she crosses to it and puts her ear against the wood, listening. "I think it's empty." As she slowly opens the door, a wave of heat flows out. Maud peers in. "It's Mister Flitch's workroom," she whispers over her shoulder.

Standing on tiptoe, I peer over her head.

The workroom is two stories in height. In the middle of it are two huge shapes draped in white canvas. The heat is coming from one of them, in pulses. But there's no fire that I can see. "What are they?" I ask.

Maud shrugs. "Some kind of machine or device," she whispers.

"Let's have a look," I whisper back.

"All right, but hurry."

Maud waits at the door while I go across the stone floor. When I reach the first shape, I duck under the canvas. It's dark under there, but my eyes can see. High overhead, I see gears, pistons, brass gleaming with bits of light leaking in from outside. There's a heavy smell of oil and hot metal.

Maud was right; it's some kind of machine, but I can't make any sense of it. It's all hunched and folded into itself. Heat pulses from it, but I can't see any fire, though it must run on coal, like the factory machines. There's a faint rumbling sound, as if gears are turning deep within it.

I want to stay and examine it further, and check to see if the other one is the same, but I know Maud will be getting impatient. When I get back to her, she leads us to a staircase. We don't make a sound going through the door at the top and into a hallway that is completely different from the factory below. There's a thick carpet on the floor and framed paintings on the walls.

"This way," Maud says, and we pad down the hallway, past doors with brass nameplates on them to a door at the end. We slip inside and close the door behind us.

Maud pulls the candle and matches from her pocket. "I'll need light to see," she says in a normal voice.

"Shouldn't you be whispering?" I whisper.

She shakes her head and strikes a match. As the candle flares, its yellow light washes over her face. "The watchman's done his rounds. He'll sit on his rump near the front door drinking tea for the next hour. We've got plenty of time."

I hope she's right. Then I turn to have a look at Mister Flitch's office.

The walls are covered in some kind of shiny red fabric. There are leather chairs scattered around, and little tables with lamps on them. At one end of the room is a massive polished desk covered with stacks of paper.

And everywhere there is gold, glimmering in the light from Maud's candle. There's gold in the picture frames, on the corners of the wooden box on the desk, on the stopper in an inkpot, woven into the patterns of the carpet on the floor. There's a fireplace that has a gilded mantelpiece, and resting on that are little statues made of gold. Over *that* is a huge portrait of Mister Flitch with a golden frame around it. He's been painted standing in front of a factory machine, holding a bolt of cloth in one hand; a pile of gold coins sits on a table next to his other hand. His gray-green eyes have a golden glint in them, and it almost looks like he is watching us. His gray-bearded face looks sour and pinched, somehow, as if he isn't very happy.

Maud has already crossed to a bookcase near the desk. Quickly she starts pulling out books—they all have pages edged in gold and the letters of their titles are stamped into the leather covers in gold. "No, no, no," she mutters, examining each one and setting it back on the shelf. "Rafi," she says, without looking away from what she is doing, "go and check the desk."

My feet sink into the lush carpet as I cross the room. The desk has three drawers on each side, with gold handles, of course, but they only have paper in them, and ink, and another book that I take to Maud. "Just a ledger," she says, "for keeping accounts. Keep looking."

The center drawer is locked.

"Any luck?" Maud asks, coming to stand next to me.

"Not really," I answer, and point to the locked drawer. "We don't have the key."

"Hmmm." Maud crouches and examines the drawer, crawling beneath the desk and knocking the underside, then peering into the keyhole. "The book must be in here." As she gets to her feet, she sees the portrait of Mister Flitch watching us.

For a moment she stares at it.

"That's him," I tell her. "Mister Flitch."

She nods. She studies the picture for another moment, then shakes her head and turns back to the desk. She yanks open one of the other drawers and pulls out a penknife—made of gold, of course. "We'll have to break the lock." And before I can protest, she shoves the knife into the lock, gives it a twist, and the drawer pops open.

The only thing in the drawer is a key. It looks heavy, about the size of my hand, and gilded along its edges in a pattern that looks almost like scales.

"Ohhhh," Maud breathes. She reaches in to pick it up. Weighing it in her hand, she turns to survey the room. "There. Bring the light."

Holding the candle, I follow her to one of the walls. She moves a low table out of the way and points. A keyhole. And then I see it—the outline of a door built right into the wall. With shaking hands, Maud puts in the key, turns it, and pushes the door open.

I follow her into the room on the other side.

The room is about half the size of the office, and it is stuffed full of things. I stand there, looking around. On one wall is a gold-framed painting of a dragon perched on a mountainside with its wings half open and fire streaming from its maw. On a table below it is a stand with some kind of curved swordlike thing resting on it.

"Wait," I say, stepping closer. "Is that a . . .?"

"Oh, Rafi," Maud says, her voice shaking, and I turn to her.

She's standing in the middle of the room. Tears gather in her eyes. "It's a collection," she whispers. "His dragon collection."

And I realize that she is right. It's not a sword on the table, it's a talon, curved, black, and wickedly sharp.

Next to the table is an open chest. I step closer to see, and Maud joins me. It's full of flat night-black platelike things with ragged edges, about as big as my hand. Maud reaches in and lifts one out. "It's a scale," she says.

My eyes are drawn back to the painting on the wall. A scale from that dragon, I guess, and so is the talon.

"This is awful," Maud says, her voice full of tears.

I can't even answer. All I can do is nod my head.

"Oh no." Maud points, and pulls me to a nearby wooden display case with a glass top. Inside it, pinned to a velvet background, is a row of tiny . . .

"What are they?" I ask, trying to see them better. They look like silvery insects. But I know they're not.

"Dragon-flies," Maud says sadly. "A kind of very tiny dragon. I've only read about them. They lived in groups of fifty or more at the edges of ponds and streams. Can you imagine how beautiful they were? Hovering over the water, glinting in the sunlight?"

I nod, because I can imagine what she's describing.

"About ten years ago they went extinct. There aren't any more like them in the world." Tears are flowing down her face now. "How could he?" she whispers. "How *could* he?"

And then I see something else. Leaving Maud, I step closer to see it better. On a small shelf is a single teacup. It's painted all over with blue flowers. My hand goes to my pocket, and I pull out the shard of teacup that I've been carrying with me since I left the Dragonfell.

Maud has come to stand beside me. "The dragon from your village," she says.

All I can do is nod, feeling a heavy weight of sadness pressing down on me.

"He must have done what the Skarth dragon said," Maud says. "He drove the Dragonfell dragon away from its lair and killed it." With a finger she gently touches the edge of the teacup. "And took its hoard." She turns to survey the room. "Is this why? Just to collect dead pieces of dead dragons?" She shakes her head. *"Why?"*

"I don't know," I manage to answer. And then I spot something. "Look," I say, pointing. On a pedestal against the opposite wall is what we came here for. Passing a shelf of eggs of all different sizes and colors, we go to the book.

It doesn't seem like anything special. It's small, covered with plain, brown leather. Like the Ratch book, its edges are singed.

Maud reaches out and opens it. "Oh my," she gasps, and leans closer. "I think a dragon must have written this by dipping its claw into ink." She turns a page, and then another that folds out into what must be a map. "Yes," she murmurs. "Very nice."

"We don't have time to read it now," I tell her, and I snap the book closed, almost catching her nose.

"Rafi!" she protests. Then she straightens and looks around at Mister Flitch's collection, and her face grows sad. "I'm glad we have the book, and the map, but I wish we'd never found this room. It's the worst place I've ever been."

I agree completely. "Let's get out of here," I say. I stow the book in the pocket of my coat, and we go out of Mister Flitch's dragon collection room and back into the office. I pinch out the candle, and we step quietly out into the hallway, closing the door of the office behind us.

Suddenly a lantern flares with light. The hallway isn't empty.

Stubb and Gringolet are there waiting for us.

CHAPTER 21

"*What* a coincidence," Gringolet says in her rough voice.
"You turning up here, Rafi Bywater, right exactly where
we want you." She stares almost hungrily at me. "Have
you made your choice yet?" Stubb looms behind her,
with his long arms folded and a sour look on his face.

Maud and I have our backs to the office door. At
Gringolet's question, which feels more like a threat, I
feel my spark begin to flare up, and I take a deep breath,
when Maud grabs my hand and squeezes it. "Just wait,
Rafi," she says quickly. "Wait."

"For what," I gasp, trying to keep ahold of myself.

"Just . . . just trust me," she says. Then she lets go of
my hand, steps forward into the light shed by their lantern, raises her chin, and speaks in a voice that is haughty

and completely unlike her. "Don't you two idiots know who I am?" she demands.

Gringolet blinks and then studies Maud over the rims of her smoked spectacles. "Never seen you before, girlie."

Stubb's eyes widen. "It's her." He elbows Gringolet in the side. "I know her, Gringy. It's Miss Flitch."

Miss *What*?

"That's right," Maud is saying. "And I order you to leave this boy alone." She points at me. "He is with me."

"I beg your pardon, miss, but we don't take orders from you, miss," Stubb says. He takes off his round hat and holds it in his hands before him, like a shield. "Just from your father, miss."

Her *father*? I stare at Maud, and I feel like my heart has dropped out of my chest and landed on the floor with a *thud*. Mister Flitch is Maud's father?

"Don't be stupid," Maud snaps. "I am acting on my father's orders, of course. And surely," she adds snidely, "his orders to his daughter supersede his orders to you, don't you think?"

"His orders to you . . . ," Stubb repeats, trying to figure it out.

"But—" Gringolet starts to say.

"So!" Maud interrupts. "Don't you dare lay a hand on me, or on him." She takes a few steps down the hallway.

I stand there, too frozen to move.

She turns and meets my eyes. *Come on*, she mouths desperately, and there's nothing else I can do but follow her, stumbling past Stubb and Gringolet, who watch us go with their mouths hanging open. Down the stairs to the main factory floor, past the iron looms. When we get to the big double doors at the front of the factory, we hear a shout and the clumping of big feet down the iron stairway. Stubb and Gringolet coming after us.

"Don't ask me any questions, Rafi," Maud says quickly. She pushes me out the doors, then takes my hand and pulls me down the front steps and across the cobbled street. "We have to get out of here."

In the alley, my four goats get to their hooves and clatter after us as we go around corners and down darkened streets, leaving the factory behind us.

When we're far enough away, I stop. Maud takes a few more hurried steps, then stops and turns back. "Come *on*, Rafi."

The goats cluster around me. The alley we're in is narrow and filled with trash and puddles, and it smells dank, like the river.

Slowly I shake my head. "You're Mister Flitch's daughter." Saying it out loud makes it even more real. "I can't believe it," I say to myself.

Maud steps closer. In the moonlight, her face looks like it's brushed with ash. She bites her lip. "Here's the thing, Rafi . . ."

I study her. "What's the thing, Maud?"

Her eyes go wide and worried. "I know you don't mean to look as if you want to skewer me, Rafi, but you do."

I don't even bother trying to make my face less fierce. "The thing is," I tell her, "that you lied to me. You've been lying to me the entire time!"

"I know!" she says. "I know, I know, I know!" Her hands are clenched into fists. "I should have told you, but I knew you wouldn't trust me as soon as I did." Then she steps closer and pokes me in the chest, and it surprises me so much that I take a step back. "And anyway, what about *you*?" she demands. "*You* have been lying to *me* just as much as I've been lying to you."

"What?" I ask.

"Even *more* maybe," she insists. "Let me ask you this, Rafi. Can you see in the dark?"

I take another step back. Oh no.

"Well? Can you?" she asks.

I nod, but then, knowing she can't see me very well in the dark alley we're in, I add, "Yes."

"And you don't feel the cold either, do you?"

"No," I grate out, and my heart begins pounding.

"Yes, I thought so," she says. "You keep forgetting to shiver."

"I'm sorry," I mutter.

"I'm a very noticing kind of person, you know," Maud says with a lift of her chin. "And you understood the Coaldowns dragon when it spoke to you, *and* the Skarth dragon." She waves a hand. "And then there are the goats. *Very* interesting, those goats, following you around like they do. And that's not all of it! That strange woman back there at the factory. Gringy?"

"Gringolet," I say dully.

"Her," Maud says with a nod. "She knew your name. She's been hunting you! And you never even thought to mention that? Or tell me what she wants with you?"

All I can do is shake my head.

"So you see, Rafi," Maud concludes, "you're just as bad as I am."

It's true. I am. Worse, maybe. Poppy pushes her nose at me and I scratch her chin and lean back against the brick wall of the alley.

Then Maud gives a trembling sigh. "No." She shakes her head. "No, that's not true. It's not the same. I might as well face up to it." She looks up, and her hazel eyes are shiny with tears. "I—I should have told you right from the start who I am. My name isn't even Maud, it's Madderlyn, though I hate that name, and yes, my last name is Flitch, and I . . . I thought I had good reasons for lying to you, but . . . well . . . maybe I didn't, really. You were just so nice, and I liked you so much, and I didn't want you to hate me. I'm very, very sorry." A tear escapes from one eye and slides down her cheek, and she turns her face away, trying to hide it. "I'm not like him, you know," she says in a tiny, sad voice. "I'm not interested in dragons because I want to collect them, or kill them, or whatever he's doing with them. I really do think they're wonderful. But you don't have to believe me, Rafi. You don't have to stay. I'm sure you could do whatever you have to do next much better without me."

She's right. I probably could do better without her. I wouldn't have a bad time of it, either. I'd have Poppy's milk, and the cold of being outdoors doesn't bother me, even though winter is coming. And I'm used to being lonely. I could easily leave her behind. All I have to do is decide to go.

Or to stay with her.

It feels like the biggest, most important decision I've ever had to make. The silence stretches out between us.

I will never, ever forget what Maud said when I asked her to tell me what she saw when she looked at me. She saw *a friend*. "You know," I say slowly, at last. "If we're going to warn the glass dragon about Mister Flitch, we'd better get started as soon as we can."

"Oh, Rafi." She rubs the tears off her face and gives me a smile as glorious as a sunrise. "You are the *best* friend, and I adore you."

I smile back at her, and it's a real smile, not a frightening one, and all of a sudden it doesn't matter that I've kept my secrets from her, and it doesn't matter about Maud lying about her father, and who knows what else, because Maud *is* my friend, a true friend to me, and I will always be true to her.

CHAPTER 22

Maud, it turns out, is a thief, too.

As we head out of the alley, she shows me a little leather bag that she stole from Mister Flitch's—from her father's—office.

"Gold, of course," she says with a sigh. "We'll be able to buy supplies." She pauses at the edge of a street and cocks her head, listening. In the distance is the sound of shouting. Gringolet and Stubb. "We'd better hide."

Creeping through the darkest alleys, the goats following, we make our way back to the riverfront.

"I don't think we can stay here for very long," Maud says when we've climbed back up the cliff to the Skarth dragon's lair. She flops down on the sand and lets out a weary sigh. "Do you know, Rafi?"

"Do I know what?" Settling on the sand beside her, I dig in a bag for a candle. When lit, the cave glows like a bowl of warm golden light. The books are stacked all around us. There's no sign of the Skarth dragon.

"You have all these . . . things about you that are strange," Maud says. "Do you know what you are?"

I nod, and take a deep breath. It's time to tell her. "I'm dragon-touched."

She sits up. "Dragon-touched? I've never heard of such a thing." She pulls her notebook out of her coat pocket. "And trust me, I've read everything there is to read about dragons. Hm. All your special powers. I suppose it makes sense."

"Does it?" I ask.

"Yes, of course it does," she says, and she sounds certain sure about it. "It's rather, well—" She shakes her head.

I give a weary nod. *Strange*, she's going to say. Or *frightening*.

"Well, you know," she goes on. "It's amazing."

"What?" I say, gaping at her.

She bursts out laughing. "Rafi, your special powers mean you can't be burned by a dragon's flames, and you wouldn't freeze in a cold mountain lair. And you can understand dragon speech. I've been studying dragons for practically my entire life, and I've read every book about dragons that I could find, but I'll never be a friend to dragons the way you are. Don't you see how lucky you are, and how wonderful it is?"

"Wonderful enough to get me blamed for a fire I didn't set," I say. "And sent away from my village, and hunted by Gringolet and Stubb."

"Yes, but look at the adventure you're having—that *we* are having. It's *so* much better than being cooped up in a—well, in a place where you don't want to be, being told how to dress and how to talk, and having a father who is, well . . ." She trails off. "Anyway, let me ask you this. How do you explain the goats?"

I shake my head. "I don't know. I like goats, that's all. And they like me."

"That is most definitely not all," she mutters, reading over a page in her book.

"There is more that I haven't told you," I say, and while she sits watching me with her hazel eyes gleaming with interest, I tell her about how the dragon called me to the highest fells when I was little, how it gave me a tiny spark—

"A *spark*?" she interrupts. Then her mouth drops open. "I saw it! Deep in your eyes when I looked, remember?"

I nod and tell her the rest of the story she interrupted, how the dragon burned my da's leg so badly, but didn't burn me.

Maud gives me a wide-eyed, solemn look. "Your da must be afraid of dragons." Then she asks the question that I've never wanted to ask myself. "If you're dragon-touched, Rafi, is he afraid of you, too?"

"I don't know. He might be, a little," I admit. "But he loves me." I glance up at her. "I'm certain sure of that."

"My father—" She frowns. "My father is the reason I became so interested in dragons. I knew that he was obsessed with them. But I didn't know about that room. I didn't know that he collected . . ." Her face looks very sad. "Rafi," she says, and her voice shakes a bit.

"Maud," I say quietly.

"Oh drat, I'm going to cry again," she mutters, blinking away tears. "Rafi, when you talk about your da . . ." She shakes her head. "Me and my father . . . we aren't like that. He doesn't love me the way your da loves you."

I get up and go to sit next to her and put my arm around her. She turns her face into my shoulder, and a moment later she's crying, and my coat is getting wet with her tears. "Dragons," she sobs. "My own father is killing dragons, Rafi. He's taking their scales and their talons, and their eggs, and their hoards. All those beautiful dragon-flies. *Why?*" she wails. "Why is he doing it?"

Her crying makes me feel like crying, too. I miss Da. I miss my village. I don't want anybody to be afraid of me. I just want to go *home*.

After a few more sniffles, Maud sits up and wipes the tears off her face with the palm of her hand, and then blows her nose on her sleeve. I give her a look, and she gives me a watery smile.

Without thinking about it, I shift to face in the direction of the Dragonfell.

Maud nods. "You do that a lot, you know. Turn toward home."

"I always know where it is," I say.

"Fascinating," she murmurs, and because she is Maud, and always thinking, she opens her red notebook and writes something down. Then she rubs her eyes. "Rafi, why, exactly, is my father hunting you?"

"He knows I'm dragon-touched," I tell her. "He wants my spark."

"*Why?*" she demands. "What for? What will he do with it?"

"I don't know," I say, shaking my head. "Gringolet said he wants me to choose between keeping my spark and saving my village. But it's not really a fair choice." In my coat pocket I still have the paper that Stubb and Gringolet nailed up outside the tavern in Barrow. Taking it out, I hand it to her.

She unfolds the paper and reads what it says. "My goodness. That's a lot of money."

"A reward?" I ask her. "For whoever captures me?"

"Oh, that's right, you can't read it," she says. "It says *Rafi Bywater, wanted for arson*—that's burning things down—*in the village of Dragonfell*." She reads on. "*Dangerous character*, and so on. Doesn't say anything about you being dragon-touched." She refolds the paper and gives it back to me. "It's not a very good picture of you."

After working for a bit longer, she yawns and mumbles to herself as she reads over what she's been writing. She's drooping with tiredness, but her brain is still going like a coal-powered steam engine. I wonder if it ever stops, even when she's asleep. She must have exciting dreams.

She looks up at me, then she blinks, as if she's seeing again how strange my face is. "Rafi, hand over the other book. I want to take a look at the map, and then . . ." She glances at her notebook. "I forget what I was going to say."

"You'll remember when you wake up," I say, and hand her a ragged blanket. "You can look at the map in the morning." Taking the blanket, she lies down on the sandy floor. Her eyes drop shut, and a moment later she's asleep. I put the candle out.

And then I wait. The stillness of the night settles around me. Without the candlelight, the cave is like a bubble of night and silence, except for the soft snores that Maud makes when she's sleeping.

A short time later, the ribbon of darkness that is the Skarth dragon flies in through the cave opening. It swoops around to land on a tall stack of books nearby, and peers down at me.

Searchers, it says.

I nod. Gringolet and Stubb know we're here in the city, somewhere. I feel a prickle of fear. "We'll leave soon," I tell the Skarth dragon. We still have a few hours until dawn, enough time for Maud to sleep. I pull the small book out of my coat pocket. "We found it in a hidden room in Flitch's office. Did you know about his collection?"

As an answer, the dragon drops off its pile of books and slithers through the air, and a second later I feel the pinpricks of its tiny claws as it lands on my arm. Clinging to my coat sleeve, it crawls toward my hand, which is holding the book. It wraps around my wrist, then snorts out a puff of smoke.

Yes… know about Flitch's collection. It fixes me with an intense stare.

I think back to the moment when I first met Mister Flitch, outside Old Shar's house in my village. He looked deep into my eyes, and he recognized what I am.

I shiver, thinking about the tiny dragon-flies pinned in the display case in Flitch's collection room.

Flitch hunts dragons. He collects them.

And now he's hunting me.

In the hour before dawn, I light the candle and then wake Maud up.

"What?" she says, her voice fuzzy with sleep.

"Time to go," I tell her.

"Oh!" She sits up, blinking, and gives me an almost shy smile. "Good morning. I want to look at the map."

"We don't have time for that now," I tell her. "The dragon says men are out searching for us. Stubb and Gringolet, probably."

"Probably," Maud agrees. "But there are just two of them, and it's a big city. We can evade them, I think." She picks up the dragon book from the sandy floor and opens it, then folds out the map. "Come look at this." She points to the map, which is only a blur to me. "We'll have to stop for supplies, then get out of the city and head north. The map shows a place called the *Ur-Lair*, and a note here says that's where the glass dragon lives."

"Ur-Lair," I repeat.

"Yes, *Ur-Lair*," she says again happily. "It's a wonderful word, isn't it? The book says it's like the original place of dragons. It should be about five days from here."

I glance toward the Skarth dragon, who is perched

on its books, watching us. "And when we get to the Ur-Lair, and warn the glass dragon, it will help us stop Mister Flitch from collecting dragons, and killing them."

Maud gives a determined nod. "That's right. We'll learn everything we need to know about dragons there, I should think."

"There's one thing I'm worried about," I tell her.

"Only one?" she asks, and raises her eyebrows.

"One other thing," I correct myself. "We've seen Gringolet and Stubb, but we haven't seen Mister Flitch. Where is he?"

"He does travel around a lot," Maud says. "To different towns and factories." She blinks several times. "And he must have been hunting dragons, too, all those times he was away."

"Anyway, if he's not here, then he might be making trouble somewhere else," I say. "He did threaten my village."

"So we need to hurry," Maud concludes.

"Yes, we do," I agree. Leaning out the cave opening in the cliff, I look down, checking to be sure it's safe to leave. The stony bank of the river glimmers in the last of the night. The goats are there, fuzzy lumps bunched together. Only Gruff is awake, standing guard over the others.

From its perch on a pile of books, the Skarth dragon

watches us with eyes that are like pinpoints of flame.

"Thank you," I say to it.

Farewell, it says, and snorts out a puff of smoke. *Farewell, Rafi of Dragonfell.*

Farewell feels like an ending, as if I'll never see the Skarth dragon again.

During the night, while Maud was sleeping, it hopped onto my knee and fixed me with an intense stare.

Youngling Rafi. It cocked its head and studied me. *Is end of dragons coming.*

"I know," I told it. "I promise I'll do whatever I can to stop it."

There was a long silence.

When the dragon spoke again, its voice sounded faded and weary. *Is likely that the end of dragons will be end of Rafi, too.*

And I knew it was right.

CHAPTER 23

While it's still dark, Maud and I climb from the cave down to the riverbank. I greet Elegance and Gruff and Fluffy, who's even fatter than ever, and I milk Poppy, and then we set off. It's still early enough, we figure, that we'll be able to sneak through the city, maybe stop to buy supplies, and be away on the road before Stubb and Gringolet can track us down.

We're wrong.

We reach the docks, which are just waking up. A man carrying a barrel gives us an odd look as we climb from the riverside path to the waterfront, followed by the goats. We pass a crane and a dark warehouse, and we're about to step out onto a street lined with shops.

"Maybe we can knock on a shop door," Maud is

saying, "and they'll open early to sell us the supplies we need." Then her eyes grow wide, and she grabs my arm and drags me into a shadowed alley. The goats bunch in behind me.

Maaaaah, Poppy complains.

"Shhhh," Maud hisses, and points.

Coming around a street corner about a block away is someone we know. Stubb. He's carrying a lantern that lights up the street, and he's leading a group of ten burly men and women. Stubb gives an order, and two men head down one street, and three more break off and go the other way. They all look keenly alert, and some of them are carrying clubs.

Maud gulps. "Rafi, those people work at my father's factory."

I see what she's saying. "They're hunting for us. How many people work for him?"

"Oh my goodness," Maud whispers. "Hundreds. Thousands." She gives her head a worried shake. "They'll be all over the city soon."

"Then we'd better get out of here," I say.

Carefully, quietly, we make our way back to the waterfront, where we sneak onto the path that runs along the river, followed by the goats. The high cliff glows white in the first light of dawn. Our feet crunch over the sand and stones.

As we walk, the cliff gets lower, and the river makes a wide turn, and as the sun rises, turning the sky gray and then pink, the city is hidden behind us. We get onto a path that winds between patches of swampland. The goats go along complaining, *maaah, maaaah, maaaaaaaah.*

"I am *soooo* hungry," Maud complains, and then laughs. "Is that what the goats are saying?"

"No," I answer. "They don't like the squishy ground under their hooves."

We walk farther until the path ends at a raised road that is paved with stone blocks.

"There you are, goats," Maud says. "You'll like this better."

She's right. After checking in both directions, we climb onto the road, the goats prancing now that they have a hard surface to walk on. The city is behind us. The swamp is on one side of the road; frozen fields are on the other, and in the distance, there are farmhouses and barns. There is a deep purple smudge in the distance. "Hills," I say, pointing. "And there's a mountain, too, beyond that." I know Maud can't see it, but I can. It rises beyond the hills, a gleaming white spire just over the horizon.

"You know, Rafi," Maud says. "We really rather desperately need supplies. And you might not feel the cold, but if we're going up a mountain I'm going to need a warmer coat and mittens and a hat. We'll have to stop in the first town we come to."

I don't like it, but I can't deny that she's right. "Maybe not the first town," I tell her, "just in case Gringolet has sent more of your father's workers after us."

Maud bites her lip and looks away. "Rafi . . . ," she begins.

I wait.

"Rafi, I want you to not call him my 'father.' Just call him 'Mister Flitch,' all right?" She gives one of her quicksilver smiles. "But you're right. We'll have to be careful." Her eyes start to sparkle. "In fact, I think we'll have to have disguises."

We walk along the road, keeping an eye out for anybody coming, and argue about how we're going to get into a town, buy supplies, and get out again, without being spotted. Even if Mister Flitch's hunters aren't in a town, I tell her, he must have had Gringolet and Stubb put up those notices with my picture on them, and I can't disguise what I am.

"Not to mention the goats," Maud adds. "They're a sure giveaway. I'll have to go into the town myself, and you can wait for me outside."

We're sitting on a grassy bank beside the road, eating the last of the dried fruit that was in the package the Skarth dragon gave us. While Maud scratches Fluffy's nose, I climb to the top of the bank and have a look around. My farseeing eyes don't even have to see that far—there's a place to buy supplies just ahead.

"There's a town around a bend in the road," I tell Maud, sliding down the bank to sit beside her.

"Oh, good," she says, giving Fluffy one more pat. "This is the fattest goat I have ever seen." Then she opens one of her bags and starts rooting around in it. "Ah," she says, and pulls out a pair of sewing scissors, which she hands to me.

"What am I supposed to do with these?" I ask.

"My disguise," she says, way too cheerfully. "Cut my hair. I'm going to be a boy. Make it short so there's no curl left."

When I'm finished cutting, she's left with a ragged black fringe that makes her hazel eyes look huge in her face. She bends and scrapes up some dirt from the ground and rubs it over her nose and cheeks to hide her freckles. Then she stands, puts on my cap, raises her chin, and folds her arms. "What do you think?"

Even with her hair chopped off and her face smudged with dirt, she's way prettier than any boy. "You don't even want to know," I tell her, climbing to my feet.

"Hmph!" she says, and digs in her bag again. She pulls out a glass square and looks into it. "I think it's an excellent disguise," she tells me.

"Is that a mirror?" I ask. I know what a mirror is, but I've never seen one before.

"Want to see?" She hands it to me.

Holding it up, I look into it, and see a strange boy—me—looking back. I hold it closer, peering into my own eyes, trying to see past the shadows to the spark that Maud saw inside me, and that Mister Flitch saw, too.

It's a frowningly fierce face, and I can see why ordinary people might be afraid of it. Maybe I *should* try smiling more.

Maud peers over my shoulder, her face reflected next to mine in the mirror. Pretty, dirt-smudged brown skin, cut-short hair.

I practice my smile on her.

"Eep!" she says, and flinches back.

I turn to face her.

She gives me a shaky smile. "Sorry, Rafi. Sorry. I forgot."

"Forgot what?" I ask, handing her the mirror.

"Well, yes, you look different," she says as she stows it away, "and a little dangerous, actually, but I don't usually see that anymore when I look at you." Then she glances up at me again. "You're a very normal boy, really."

"Normal?" I say skeptically.

"Truly," she says, and starts down the road toward the town. The goats and I follow. "You're kind, and brave, and stubborn, and you're awfully nice, and you're . . ." She shrugs. "Normal."

When we get to the edge of the town, I sit down behind a low stone wall to wait while Maud goes in to buy supplies.

"Be careful," I warn her as she sets off.

"Oh, Rafi," she scoffs. "Of course I'll be careful."

But she's not careful enough.

CHAPTER 24

The goats settle in a sunny spot, napping, and I sit with my back against the wall, waiting . . .

. . . and thinking about being *normal* . . .

. . . and worrying about the Dragonfell . . .

. . . and half falling asleep.

And then I hear a distant shriek. I sit up, eyes wide, heart suddenly pounding. Leaping to my feet, I look toward the cluster of cottages. Puffs of smoke are coming from the center of the town.

Something's wrong.

"Come on, goats," I shout, and start running toward the town, along the rutted dirt road. Panting, I pass the first cottages, and then a few more, and then the road widens and becomes a town square paved with stone.

Parked in the center of it are two vaporwagons, the steam-driven cars I'd seen near Skarth. They have a set of tall spoked wheels in the back, and smaller wheels in the front, and are gleaming with riveted brass and emerald-green paint. One of them is belching out clouds of black smoke from a tall smokestack.

And beside them, Maud is facing three figures. One of them—it's Gringolet—is gripping her by the arm, and Maud is struggling. I catch a glimpse of a hand dealing a heavy blow, knocking Maud to the ground.

I'm already halfway across the square, bearing down on Gringolet and her two men—me, a kid, against three grown people—but I can't let them hurt Maud—and with that thought I feel the spark inside me kindle into flame.

"Rafi," Maud shrieks.

—and the shadows swoop around me and my steps grow heavier as if I'm shaking the ground as I stride, and from the corners of my eyes I see sparks streaming away from me, and flames. Gringolet, turning, sees me and screeches out a high, grating cry. Her men stumble away. I go after them. My hand reaches from the shadows swirling around me, and with strength that comes from somewhere—I don't know where—I seize the front of one of the men's shirt and hurl him across the square, and he slams into a cottage wall and falls onto the ground like a bundle of rags. He drags himself to his feet and runs. The other man scurries away, too.

"Get the others!" Gringolet screams after them.

Then she whirls to face us—and takes a step toward Maud.

"Leave her ALONE!" I roar, and Gringolet flinches away.

I take another step, and she flees into a nearby street, shouting for her men.

Maud climbs to her feet, looking wildly around her. Quickly she grabs up a bag and hurls it into one of the vaporwagons.

What is she *doing*?

She picks up another bag, and then starts climbing into the vaporwagon.

Then I spot Gringolet pulling out the long, sharp pin from her sleeve, and her two men, and they've brought reinforcements, more of the burly workers, all armed with clubs and knives. They start across the square toward me.

"Make your choice, Rafi Bywater!" Gringolet shouts. "Come with us, and we'll leave the girl alone, and your village, too!"

I feel my spark flare, and I take a step toward them. Ten men is a lot, but I can fight them.

"Rafi!" Maud shouts, and I glance toward her. Her

face is bruised, and blood is trickling from her nose. "Come *on!*"

I take a steadying breath. Then another, shaking, wrapping my arms around myself, willing my sparks and shadows to go back where they came from. Then I whirl and race toward the vaporwagon, and climb over its tall back wheel and inside.

As I climb in, I see a dashboard covered with dials and knobs and little brass flywheels. Below that is a small closed iron door that pulses with heat; at the front is a huge brass boiler lined with rivets, and the tall smokestack puffing out black smoke.

Maud is bent, stuffing the bags under a polished wooden bench. She slides over. "Get in, get in," she pants.

"I'm in," I gasp. "Go! Make it go!"

Maud sits up, pointing. "Pull that lever," she orders.

I pull the nearest lever toward me. Nothing happens.

"The other way!" Maud shouts.

I glance up to see Gringolet and her men bearing down on us, rushing across the village square.

"Gah!" Maud shrieks. "Go!"

With all my strength, I shove the lever, and with a rattle-clash, the vaporwagon starts to move. Pistons pump, and the wheels turn. Black smoke gusts from its smokestack. The vaporwagon bumps over the cobblestones, straight toward one of the cottages, picking up speed.

"How do we steer it?" I shout over the rattle of the steam engine.

Instead of answering, Maud leans past me to yank on another lever, and the vaporwagon turns at the last second, barely missing the cottage. We clatter across the square, past Gringolet, who is shouting orders at her men, and Maud steers us onto the road.

I turn and kneel on the seat to see behind us. Gringolet and her men are piling into the other vaporwagon, ready to come after us. My goats are trotting across the square. Fat Fluffy is falling behind. "My goats!" I yell.

"Oh my goodness gracious!" Maud gasps, and leans across to throw the lever again, and our vaporwagon slows, then rolls to a stop. "Hurry, Rafi. *Hurry!*"

"Goats!" I call, and they trot up the road toward us.

Back in the square, Gringolet's vaporwagon shudders, and then roars to life with a cloud of pitch-black smoke.

Behind the seat I'm kneeling on is a long bin half filled with coal. "Up here!" I call to the goats. Nimbly, Poppy and Elegance leap onto the step, then up onto the mound of coal. Then comes Gruff, with a clatter of hooves that scratch the green paint. I leap to the ground and boost Fluffy up. With a flail of her legs, she finds her footing and joins the others.

Maud is practically vibrating with her need to be off.

I climb back in, and before I'm even sitting on the bench beside her, she throws the lever and we zoom away, just as Gringolet's vaporwagon starts racing toward us.

Maud glances over her shoulder, then at me, and gives one of her sudden grins. Her cheek is bruised where Gringolet hit her. "I've never driven one of these things before," she shouts, over the loud rattle-clash of the steam engine.

I check on Gringolet, coming up the road behind us. "They're getting closer," I shout back.

"Then we'd better go faster!" Maud turns one of the little flywheels. "That should wake up the fire a bit. Now add some more coal to the firebox. There should be some gloves around here someplace."

"I don't need gloves," I remind her, and grab a long-handled shovel from behind the seat. She points at the iron door, and I open it, feeling the heat of the metal under my bare hands. The coal fire inside is blindingly, brilliantly white-orange; a wave of heat gusts out, making Maud flinch away.

Quickly I shovel in more coal and slam the door again. I stow the shovel and check on the goats.

Gringolet's vaporwagon has fallen farther behind. I can see her driving, and all ten of her men clinging to the side of the wagon, or riding on the pile of coal in the back.

As I watch, Gringolet's vaporwagon bucks, bumps, and lurches to a stop, surrounded by steam.

"They threw a piston," Maud says with a glance over her shoulder.

"Whatever that means," I say.

"They'll have to stop to fix it." She gives a satisfied nod. "It'll take them all day to get the parts they need. We'll get way ahead of them."

But we can't truly get away. The problem with the vaporwagon is that we have to stay on the road. As long as we follow the road, they'll know exactly where we're going.

CHAPTER 25

We drive for a long way without another sign of Gringolet and her hunters coming up from behind. We pass farms and a few small villages, and for a while the road runs alongside a river. My bottom is sore from bouncing on the hard wooden seat, and my ears echo with the sound of the engine chug-a-chugging away. Every now and then I have to throw more coal on the fire.

"It boils the water to make steam," Maud shouts over the rattle and bang, "and the steam does things in the engine to make it go, but I don't know what, exactly." She casts a glance over her shoulder at the bin behind the seat. "I hope we don't run out of coal."

Then she shows me how to steer, by turning the

lever, which she calls a *tiller*. "I want to have a look at the dragon book and the map," she says, pulling it out of her coat pocket. She wedges herself into a corner of the seat, with her feet propped against the dashboard, and tries to steady the book enough to read it. The wheels go over an extra-large bump in the road, and Maud makes a face. "Ow," she says, and puts her hand over her mouth. "I bit my tongue."

Late in the afternoon, she decides it's time to stop. She checks the map one more time, and points at a clump of trees well off the road. "I think that's it." She drives off the road and turns a brass flywheel, and the vapor-wagon chugs to a stop. The engine idles, and slow puffs of smoke come from the smokestack.

"Phew!" she says in the sudden quiet. "Rafi, I'll drive on a bit and park in the trees over there. Can you hide our tracks leading off the road?"

"Yep," I answer, and I'm glad to jump down onto the springy grass. The goats join me.

Maud drives away, and I scuff out the place where we left the road, and then drag some dead branches over where our wheels turned onto the grass. Looking around, I take a deep breath and realize how far we've come. The river and the cliffs and Skarth are far behind us, and ahead are forested hills that pile up on each other, and looming beyond them are steep, snow-covered slopes leading to one huge, cone-shaped mountain. The Ur-Lair. Seeing it makes my heart pound and my breath come short. The spark inside me burns hot and keen.

With the goats trotting behind me, I run over a low hill to the clump of trees where Maud is waiting. As I approach, our vaporwagon gives off one more big puff of black smoke and goes quiet.

Maud hops down holding the book with the map unfolded.

"It won't be dark for an hour," I say as I come up to her. "We could have kept going and gotten closer to the Ur-Lair."

"We had to stop," Maud says, and opens another fold of the map. "There's a dragon village near here." She turns and surveys the low hills all around us. "Just over that rise there, if the map is correct. At the very least we can warn the dragon there about my . . . about Mister Flitch and his collection."

She's right.

Maud consults the map again, then folds it up and stows the book in her pocket. "This way!" she says, and leaving the goats behind in the copse of trees, we hike along the base of a hill. About halfway around we hit a narrow path that leads through another small forest—I've never been surrounded by trees before, and it makes me feel strangely small. We follow the path for a long way, until we come out of the trees and head up the side of a low hill.

"Wait," I say, and grab Maud's arm. "Listen."

She stops, and we stand in the middle of the path.

In the distance I can hear a high jingling sound, and a lower ringing, and then a ripple of chimes.

Maud looks at me, eyes sparkling, "Do you know what it is?"

"Bells?"

"Wait and see," she says, and we go on. The path crests the hill and in a bowl between this rounded, grassy hill and two others, is a village. It's a cluster of whitewashed cottages, and it's where the ringing is coming from.

As we go closer, I see bells hanging from the eaves of every house. They're made of iron, of tarnished silver, of brass, from the size of a blueberry, to the size of an egg, and even bigger. Chimes tinkle in the breeze. The biggest bell is set in a high tower at the center of the village.

"Isn't it wonderful?" Maud asks, smiling.

I'm about to agree, but then I realize.

There are no people.

And half of the cottages are burned out.

We come to the first house. The door is open, and the windows are broken, and all of it is charred black from a fire. The yard is overgrown with a rosebush that sprawls out into the path. The next cottage is just as burned and abandoned.

We go to the center of the village. From the bell in the tower hangs a frayed rope. Maud gives it a tug, and a deep, desolate *bong* rings out, echoing from the surrounding hills.

She gulps and consults the book, then looks back up at me. "It hoarded bells, of course," she says softly. "And shared them with the people who lived in its village."

I nod. "Where?"

She checks the map. "That's where it laired," she says, pointing to one of the hills.

Without speaking, we climb the hill where the bell-hoarding dragon laired. The whole top of it is bald, scraped down to bare rock. In the middle is a pile of stones, and around it are bells, all half melted. The stone itself is scorched black.

"Maud," I whisper, pointing.

She turns to look. Just over the crest of the hill is what appears to be a tunnel made of a row of curved pillars that meet in a knobbed arch. Beyond it is a huge, white boulder with . . . with spikes all over it.

It's not an arched tunnel, it's a rib cage, and it's not a boulder, it's a skull. It's a dragon skeleton. Huge, way bigger than the Coaldowns dragon.

"Oh, I see." With shaking fingers, Maud folds the map back into the book, and closes it, and very carefully puts it back into her pocket. "We're too late," she whispers. "He got here first."

As we walk back through the half-burned, abandoned village, Maud stops, looking down at the path, but I don't think she's seeing it. "Rafi," she whispers.

"I know," I say, stepping up beside her, and putting my arm around her shoulders. She's thinking about her father again, knowing that he's killed the thing that she loves most: a dragon.

Gringolet must have done it for him. Maybe she did it before she gave up her own spark. When she was dragon-touched, she couldn't be burned by a dragon's flame, so she could get right up close to it and kill it.

Maud leans into me, and I can feel her shaking. "What do you think he collected from the bell dragon?"

"I didn't see any bells in his collection room," I say.

"Neither did I." She sighs. "It must have been something else."

Realization slams into me. "Their spark," I say, feeling

stupid that I didn't realize it before.

Maud turns and looks up at me. "*You* have a spark, Rafi. But dragons have a lot more than that. Don't they?"

I nod. "But I'm betting that's what he really wants from them. Their fire." I think it through. "Their power."

"Why?" Maud whispers. "Why, why, why? That's the question."

I don't know the answer.

In silence we follow the trail back. The sun dips down behind the hills, and as night falls the air grows damp and cold.

Our campsite is a small clearing in the trees. The vaporwagon is parked nearby, and the goats are all inside it, sleeping in the coal bin, which they like better than sleeping on the soft, grassy ground.

After rummaging in her bag, Maud pulls out a candle and lights it.

I get busy unpacking our dinner, the sorts of things that Maud picked out without worrying about the cost because she had a purse full of gold to pay for it. In the glimmering light of the candle, we eat hothouse grapes, and bread and soft cheese, and cubes of spiced meat, and boiled eggs with pepper, and sugar-dusted nut pastries, only a little squished from being in the bag.

When we've finished eating, Maud flops on her back

with her hands on her stomach. "What a feast." She sighs contentedly. "Rafi, I know we're in big trouble, that Gringolet is hunting us, and I'm terribly sad about the bell dragon, and about my . . . about Mister Flitch, but I can't help it. I'm about as happy as I've ever been in my life right now."

"Why?" I ask. I sit cross-legged on the grass, watching her.

"Just . . . being here. Knowing that you know the truth about me now, which is *such* a relief. Knowing that I'm about to find out all the dragons' secrets."

"And that we can help save them," I add.

"Yes, that too." She sits up again and pulls the dragon book out of her coat pocket. "Listen to this, Rafi." She finds her place on the page and starts reading aloud.

A dragon hoard is the thing that the dragon must have.
Each dragon hoards a different thing. Such as:

mouses
clear pieces of glass for looking through
also mirrors
teacups with blue flowers
tinkly bells
books

spiders
pocket watches
sea glass
silver spoons
mittens and other knitted things
drawings of pretty flowers

"Do you see what this list means, Rafi?" she asks, looking up at me. "There are a lot more dragons out there. I mean, he can't have found them all, can he?"

I hope not. "Does it say anything about people who are dragon-touched?" I ask.

"Not yet," she answers, turning a page. "But the handwriting is very difficult to decipher." She smiles. "Or claw-writing, I should say, since a dragon wrote this." She moves the candle nearer to see better. It's almost burned to a stub. "There is a bit in here about lairs, too."

Peering closer, she turns another page, and with her elbow, knocks the candle over.

It drops to the ground and goes out.

I see her blinking in the sudden darkness.

"Ohhhh," she whispers. "That was very, very stupid."

"What?" I ask.

She turns her face toward me, but I know it's too dark for her to see me.

"Rafi, I used our last match to light the candle."

"So?" I ask.

"Without a match to fire the engine, we won't be able to start the vaporwagon in the morning. Rafi, we're *stuck!*"

CHAPTER 26

Neither of us sleeps much during the night. Maud's probably imagining Gringolet and her hunters coming up the road, maybe with reinforcements. Maybe even Mister Flitch himself is coming.

I'm lying awake thinking about coal-powered, steam-driven engines.

I get up just as the sky is turning pink, and gray light sifts into our campsite. Maud sits up, yawning and rubbing her eyes.

The goats are clustered near the vaporwagon, grazing, and . . . instead of four, there are *six* of them! One of them is much skinnier than she was before—during the night, fat Fluffy gave birth to two little kids. One is black and the other is white, and they have blunt baby-goat faces and tiny hooves.

"Oh!" says Maud, going to crouch and hold a hand out to the two kids. "Oh, Rafi, look! They're so, so cute!" The white one wobbles closer. "He's so little!"

I bend to look more closely. "Yes, she is."

"And her adorable sister." She leans to peer around Fluffy's flank where the other kid is hiding.

"Her brother," I tell her.

Maud beams. "Well then, we'll name the white one, the girl, Cloud. And the black one . . ."

I crouch down to have a better look at him, then nod. "He'll be Coal."

Coal and Cloud wobble over to Fluffy, who stands; the babies duck their heads under her belly and start nursing at her udder. Their tails waggle happily as they drink.

While they nurse, I milk Poppy and give Maud the first cup, then get some more. The warm goat milk is delicious, but it makes me miss my da, and I blink away a wave of missing the Dragonfell.

Maud stands with hands on hips, looking in dismay at the two big bags full of food and her winter gear. "This is going to be a lot to carry. And the baby goats won't be able to walk far." She glares at the vaporwagon. "I can't *believe* I let the flame go out."

"Well," I say slowly. "I have an idea about that."

"Rafi, Gringolet can't be that far behind us," she reminds me. "And Mister Flitch has threatened your village. We have to hurry."

"Certain sure we do," I respond. "But just let me think about this for a bit."

With a shrug, she sits down, opens the dragon book, and starts to read.

And I go to inspect the vaporwagon.

It's a big, gleaming beast of a machine, but . . .

. . . as I look it over, it starts to make sense to me.

Front wheels, for steering. Directly ahead of the driver's seat is the firebox, and over that is the boiler, full of water. When it's burning, the coal fire heats the water, making steam. I climb into the driver's seat to have a better look. Yes, there is a gleaming brass pipe leading from the boiler, and down. The dashboard's gauges and knobs and flywheels—I can see how each of them work. There's a little glass tube half full of water—it shows that the boiler still has plenty of water in it. A pull on a knob sends extra grease into all the moving parts of the engine. I open the blower valve so the fire will get plenty of air. A quick glance at the bin behind the seat shows that we have lots of coal left. I grab the shovel and load up the firebox.

Now for a spark. I kneel by the firebox door and peer

in. The shiny black coal is mounded on a grate in the bottom of it. I reach in with my hand and rearrange the coal so it'll burn well.

And Maud pokes her nose in. "What're you *doing*, Rafi? The fire's out and we don't have any matches. There's no way to start it."

I turn to give her a long look.

She stares.

I know what she sees in my eyes.

"Oh my," she gasps. "Yes, I see. Go. Do it."

I have a spark inside me. It has flared up before, when I've been angry, or when I've been protecting somebody or something that I love. Maybe I can use it now.

I concentrate. Shadows close in around me. Deep in my chest, right next to my heart, I feel the click, and then the flare as my spark bursts into flame.

"Eep!" Maud says, and disappears.

I focus on the coal in the firebox. Coal is rock; it shouldn't be easy to light, but the spark in me speaks to it. There's a white-hot flash, and a moment later the firebox is pulsing with orange and yellow flame, the air wavery with heat. I withdraw my hand, close the firebox door, and get to my feet.

"It's all right, Maud," I call.

Her face appears again at the side of the vaporwagon. Her eyes are shining. "Oh, Rafi! Well done!"

I grin at her. Anybody else would be running away from somebody like me, but not Maud, who thinks I'm *normal.*

"Come on, goats!" she calls, and hands me an overstuffed bag. We get them loaded up, including Fluffy with her babies, along with our supplies, and drive the vaporwagon back onto the road.

We drive for most of the morning without seeing anyone. The hills get closer, and so does the mountain where the glass dragon is. I'm taking a turn at the tiller, while Maud tries to read from the dragon book.

As we drive along, I can't stop thinking about how the vaporwagon works. Maybe the spark in me calls to the heat and power in the engine. Steam expanding, driving the pistons, turning the wheels. All its parts fit together so perfectly.

It makes me wonder about the huge machines we saw in Mister Flitch's workroom, the ones covered with canvas. One of them was pulsing with heat and power. I don't think they were vaporwagons, and they weren't factory machinery . . .

"Rafi!" Maud's shout interrupts me.

I blink and glance over at her.

She's frowning. "Stop for a moment," she shouts over

the loud clatter-rattle of the engine.

I pull back the throttle, set the damper on the firebox, and the vaporwagon comes to a stop with a quiet *chuff-chuff-chuff*.

"Look." She points. "Is there something on the road ahead of us?"

To her eyes it must be just a blur. But I can see, as the road curves, heading into the hills, that there's a big vaporwagon puffing black smoke. I squint, and bring it into focus. Driving it is a familiar, ashy-gray figure gleaming with pins.

"Gringolet," I say grimly.

"Oh no." Maud clenches her fists. "She must have gotten ahead of us during the night."

I climb up to stand on the bench. From here, shading my eyes, I can see more. Riding in the back of Gringolet's vaporwagon are a lot of men, really tough-looking ones, wearing leather suits that look like they might be fireproof. After that comes another pair of vaporwagons pulling three carts hitched together, carts that are carrying something huge covered with canvas cloth. I recognize it. It's one of the giant machines from Mister Flitch's workroom.

I turn and drop back onto the bench beside Maud. My thoughts are whirring like a steam engine's gears.

That machine. They're bringing it up the mountain, to the Ur-Lair. Mister Flitch built it. Is it a weapon for fighting dragons?

If it is, there's something missing.

If the machine is steam-driven and coal-powered, then where is the coal to make it go?

And this is just *one* of the mysterious machines that we saw in Mister Flitch's workroom.

Where is the other one?

CHAPTER 27

Gringolet's convoy is moving fast. As I watch, the heavy vehicles turn off the main road and onto a rougher dirt road that leads toward the Ur-Lair mountain.

Maud pulls our bags from under the seat and flings them to the ground. "Hurry *up*," she chides.

I'm staring at the Ur-Lair again. Halfway up the mountain is a tree line, and above that are steep slopes that are gray-ash covered here and there with patches of snow.

Maud pulls at my arm, and I blink and look at her. "Did you hear me, Rafi? I said that if we hurry, we can beat Gringolet to the mountain." She points. "The road curves, but we can go straight there."

Yes. Straight there. I close the damper and feel the fire

inside our vaporwagon flicker out. A last bit of smoke and steam leak from the engine.

I leap to the ground, joining Maud and the goats.

The goats. The mountain is no place for them.

Actually, it's a perfect place for goats, but not a mountain that might be inhabited by a big, hungry dragon. I point at Gruff, the big billy. "Stay here," I order. Then I grab both of the bags from Maud and set off, heading into the forest of thick, snow-dusted pine trees that covers the lower hills. At first it's not too steep, but it's not long before the footpath we're on heads straight up, one switchback after another. I can hear Maud panting as she tries to keep up, but I can't slow down.

"Ra—" she gasps, "fi!"

"What!" I ask.

We get to a switchback, and I make the turn and keep climbing up, but Maud pauses, then leans over with her hands on her knees, trying to catch her breath. "You might," she pants, "not have noticed, but . . ." She straightens and shakes her head. "It's gotten dark."

I look around. It *is* dark. Night. A glow off to the east shows that the moon is not far from rising.

"I'm not sure I have much hiking left in me," Maud says wearily.

I want to keep going. I *could* keep going. But I'm not leaving Maud behind. "All right," I say, and my voice sounds rough. "We can stop. Gringolet won't be able to drive the vaporwagons over that road in the dark. She'll have to stop for the night, too."

We hike a little farther, to the ragged line where the pine trees give way to the ashy slope. Maud stands there with her hands on her hips, looking up at the dark cone shape that is the Ur-Lair mountain.

"Maud," I ask her, dropping the bags to the ground. "Do you know what those big machines were, the ones we saw in Mister Flitch's workroom?"

"No idea," she answers. "He's always tinkering with the factory machines, I know that much. He's almost as interested in them as he is in dragons."

"Gringolet is bringing one of them to the Ur-Lair," I tell her. "It was loaded on carts pulled by the other vaporwagons. Don't you think it could be some kind of weapon?"

Maud blinks. "Yes, it very well could be," she says soberly.

Quietly we set up camp and eat the rest of the food. It isn't long before Maud yawns. "G'night, Rafi," she murmurs, lies down, and falls asleep as soon as her eyes close.

I can't sleep. The spark inside me is burning too hot, making me twitchier than I've ever felt before, making my skin feel like it doesn't quite fit me right. I get to my feet and pace around the little clearing we're in. I pause to pull a blanket out of a bag and tuck it around Maud, and then keep pacing. The air is chilly and crisp. After a while, the moon comes up, edging over the points of the pine trees.

I turn to look at the mountain. Maud and I are camped at the very edge of the tree line, with thick forests of pines below us. Above us, steep, snow-covered slopes glimmer in the moonlight.

As I stand there I have a strange thought. In a way, Mister Flitch hoards dragons. Maybe he's obsessed with them, just like Maud is, but in a twisted way. I remember how Flitch looked at me, when he saw the spark deep in my eyes. He looked greedy. Even then he wanted my spark. But when he took Gringolet's spark from her, he didn't keep it for himself. What did he do with it?

Standing there in the velvety darkness, I gaze up toward the Ur-Lair. From where I'm standing it looks like somebody took a giant knife and used it to slice off the very top of the mountain, leaving a ragged edge like the wall around a castle. I can see a fainter line, which is the road leading up to it. That's the way that Gringolet will go, with the huge machine. To beat it up there, Maud and I will have to start climbing as soon as the sun rises. For now, the moon is riding high, spilling silvery light over the slopes of the mountain.

As I watch, two shapes appear at the very edge of the

mountaintop and launch themselves into the air. They drop and then glide, only dark shadows, and then I catch a glimpse of moonlight on scales, silver at the edge of a sweep of wings, the gleam of a fiery eye.

Dragons.

Trembling all over, I watch them fly. Seeing them makes me feel brimful of excitement and fright and a strange kind of exultation. They are *dragons*! They are so mighty, and so glorious, they make me want to leap into the sky and fly with them, wingtip to wingtip.

They fly silently, part of the night. They circle above the road, and I know they're spying out Gringolet and her men and the canvas-covered shape that is the mystery machine. Their circle widens, and they pass overhead, huge, silent, dark shapes, gliding, and then one of them beats its wings, and a rush of wind buffets the pines. For a moment they are silhouetted against the snowy slopes, and then they fly up and over the lip of the mountain and are gone.

For the rest of the night, I pace around our campsite, waiting for morning.

At last, the sky turns pearly, and the snowy sides of the mountain turn pink, and I'm about to wake Maud up when I see something at the rim of the lopped-off mountaintop. Dragon. It perches there for a second, tiny in the distance, and then launches itself into the air. It sweeps along the slopes, kicking up whirls of ash and snow behind it, plunging down, and down, and then it looms closer, getting bigger and bigger, and with a heart-thumping gasp, I realize that it's coming straight toward me.

CHAPTER 28

The dragon lands next to our campsite with a ground-shaking *thump* and a swirl of dry ash that settles around it like silver-glinting dust.

Behind me I hear a rustle, Maud sitting up, and then a high-pitched *meep!* as she catches sight of the dragon.

I step forward to meet it.

The dragon is twice the size of the Coaldowns dragon, and it looms over me. Its scales are a deep indigo shading to glittering black on its legs; its wings are a lighter purple, poised half open over its back as if it's ready to take off again. Its spiky crest runs like a row of knives from the top of its head to the tip of its barbed tail; its eyes are black, with a spark deep within. It smells of ice and cold stone and the thin mountain air, but it pulses with heat, melting the snow around it.

I stare up at it, my heart pounding, but before I can say anything, it lunges toward me, opening its wings with a clap, launching itself from the ground at the same time, and snatches me up.

"Rafi!" Maud screams, and then I can't hear anything more because the wind is ripping past my ears. The dragon swoops low over the forest. Its claw clutches my chest, and my legs are dangling; one of my shoes falls off, and I watch it tumble down, disappearing into the pine trees. Then the dragon banks, and pumps its wings, and the wind thunders by again as it climbs past the slopes. I catch a glimpse of the mountaintop, and we're over its rim, and I see the Ur-Lair laid out below me.

The whole top of the mountain is hollowed out, like a bowl made of rock. Or a nest. And it's full of dragons.

What are they doing here? A dragon hates to leave its lair—I know that. But then I realize. Mister Flitch has destroyed their lairs, driving them out. They are hiding here. I have enough time to see a huge, pink-tinged dragon in the center of the nest, and around it are dragons that are the same purple as the one carrying me, and other dragons that are big and small, and lots of different colors, and there's a wide pool of water with more dragons in it, and then the dragon carrying me folds its wings, and my stomach drops as we plummet downward.

The stone floor gets closer and closer, and the dragon banks, and drops me. I fall a few feet, and the dragon pulls up with a *whoosh* and a whirl of dust, and settles nearby.

I get to my feet, one shoe on, and one sock, and look around. The high, curving walls of the Ur-Lair tower above me. Overhead is the circle of the sky, still pink with dawn. My breath is fizzing in my lungs, and I feel my spark fully aflame in my chest.

I am surrounded by dragons. They are all crowding closer, craning their heads to see me. I stand still and let them come.

There's the purple-black dragon who brought me here, shaking out its wings and folding them neatly on its back. Next to it is a smaller dragon with faded white scales, a slim body, four claws, and a gray-tinged mane that floats in tendrils around its head. Another dull red dragon the size of a horse has wings, forelegs, and a snakelike tail. A deep green dragon slithers from the pool and crawls over the stone floor, dripping with water; it has fins instead of wings, and no teeth. Farther away I see two other water dragons peering at me from their pool, and a red-crested, dark brown dragon who is curled around a hoard of silver spoons, and a bigger pale blue dragon with two heads that look like they're arguing with each other as it lurches closer.

They are all staring at me. The dragons are all different sizes and shapes and colors, but their eyes are the same—they are shadow dark, and a flame burns deep within each one.

The ground shakes under my feet. From behind me I hear a shift of scales over scales, and a hot *whumph* of breath. I spin around to see the biggest dragon of them all. I wish Maud were here with me. She'd be scared, I think, but she'd be fascinated, too, and whipping out her red book to take notes. The big dragon steps closer, its claws gouging the stone floor of the Ur-Lair, until it looms over me.

It is the glass dragon. Its scales are clear, tinted a sun-dappled pink, and its wings are crystal edged with ruby, and its crest flows in ragged shards from its head to its tail. Deep within it, I can see its spark, a faintly glowing molten core of flame.

With a sound like a groan, the glass dragon settles onto the ground, and then it cranes its neck down until its huge head is hanging right in front of me. I smell the hot thunder and lightning smell radiating from its scales, and feel the rush of its breath ruffling my hair as it sniffs me. Then it cocks its head, examining me from head to foot.

I should be frightened. But I'm not.

"Hello," I say to it.

At the sound of my voice, all of the other dragons

flinch back a little, and then they draw closer to hear. The dull red dragon even lies down like a dog, resting its head on its front paws, its snaky tail curled behind it.

What is it? one of the heads of the two-headed blue dragon asks, peering down at me.

Shhhhh, hisses the other head.

Both heads, I realize, are wearing woolen hats with pompons on them. Maud read it in the dragon book's list of hoards: *mittens and other knitted things.* They have scarves wrapped around their snaky necks, too.

The other thing I realize is that all the dragons, even the indigo one, are old, and their sparks are not as bright as they should be. Not as old and decrepit as the Coaldowns dragon, but not a whole lot younger, either.

I take a deep breath and say loudly, "I am Rafi. I am dragon-touched. And I'm here to warn you."

Ahhhhh, breathes the glass dragon. It reaches out with a huge foreleg, and with the tip of a claw, it turns me around so it can see me from all sides.

It warns us? asks the water dragon in a drippy voice.

It warns us of the Flitch? the dull red dragon asks.

"Yes," I answer.

The big indigo dragon who fetched me makes a snorting sound, and a billow of white smoke erupts from its nostrils. *Dragons know more of the Flitch than this creature does.*

"No, you don't," I say, turning to look at them all. "One of Flitch's hunters, Gringolet, is bringing a machine here, to the Ur-Lair. I think it might be a weapon, for killing dragons."

At my words, the dragons murmur to each other, and eye me as if I'm a bug, or something they could step on if it says anything else they don't like.

The indigo dragon reaches out with its forefoot, and before I can duck away, it puts its claw through the cloth of my coat and lifts me into the air. I struggle like a worm on a fish hook, and it suddenly gives me a shake that makes all my bones knock together, and drops me onto the hard stone floor of the Ur-Lair. *It knows nothing.* Its voice sounds scornful. *It is too small and soft and squishy and stupid.*

I scramble to my feet. The indigo dragon isn't wrong. I feel a sharp bolt of despair. I'm a kid. What can I actually *do* to help the dragons? What if . . . What if I can't do anything? A little corner of my mind is worried about Maud, too. She's down there alone on the side of the mountain. I hope she's not too frightened.

And then the flame in me flares up again, and I glare at the indigo dragon. My fists clench. "Listen," I shout at it. "Flitch is dangerous. He's driving dragons out of their lairs and . . . and collecting them. He's collecting their sparks, their flames. He'll destroy you all, every one of you."

The indigo dragon glares back at me. *Think you that we do not know this?* It snorts out another cloud of white smoke, but I hold my ground.

Then the dawn-pink glass dragon makes a rumbling sound and surges to its feet. *Your flame burns so brightly,* it says to me, *but you do not see. Come now, youngling. Come see this dragon's hoard.*

CHAPTER 29

The glass dragon lumbers around, and the other dragons open a path for it. It's as big as a ship under full sail, with all flags flying, and I'm a little boat following in its wake. It leads me to the edge of the Ur-Lair, where the stone floor meets the walls in a smooth curve. The dragon settles there, curling its tail around a big wooden chest. With a claw tip, it opens the chest.

See? it asks.

I step over the tip of its tail and look into the box. It is lined with green velvet, and displayed on the velvet . . .

I reach out, then stop and glance up at the dragon. It is watching me, and I can see the fire in its deep, shadowy eye. "Can I?" I ask.

Yes, it answers.

I reach into the box and take up part of the dragon's hoard. It is a circular, polished piece of glass about the size of my hand. A lens. For looking through, and seeing more clearly. I return it to its place. Next to it is a mirror, backed with silver and reflecting the sky, which has turned blue with morning. The chest is full of other lenses and mirrors and a few pairs of spectacles.

Oh. "I don't have a propitiation for you," I say to the glass dragon.

It cocks its head. *Dragon-touched, brightly burning,* it asks, and its voice sounds like the ringing of bells, *what do you see? What is a dragon?*

I'm not sure what to say. Maud would have an answer. She could pull out her red notebook and tell them everything she knows. The other dragons have gathered nearby, listening. "A dragon is big and powerful," I say slowly. Then I remember the Skarth dragon. "Or it can be tiny and a little cranky. Or weary, like the Coaldowns dragon." I remember what the Ratch book said about dragons, how they were evil. I remember that my da was burned by a dragon.

I gaze up at the glass dragon, and I can see—*this* is what a dragon is. Huge and glorious. Not something that can be collected by a man like Mister Flitch. It lowers its head until I can look right into its eyes. Its spark is in there, deep inside. It hoards mirrors and lenses. "What do you see?" I whisper.

With a claw tip it hooks a mirror from its hoard, and holds it up in front of its big eye, looking into it. *Dragon*, it says. The mirror looks tiny in its enormous claw. Then it reaches down, holding out the mirror to me. *Does it see clearly?* it asks. *Does it see what a dragon is?*

I take the mirror. It's perfectly round, and as smooth as a pool of water. I hold it up and look into it. It's my face, just as I saw it in a mirror before, when Maud disguised herself.

What are you? the glass dragon asks.

I peer into the mirror. My hair is the bright crimson and gold of burning embers.

What are you? the glass dragon asks again.

My mouth is set and stern, and the lines of my face are fierce.

Can you see what you are? the dragon asks a third time.

And I stare into my eyes. My dark, dark eyes that Tam Baker's-Son said were full of shadows, and that Maud said looked like they drew in the light. I still remember how she leaned close and peered into my eyes and said softly, "There's a spark in there, Rafi."

My eyes are not the eyes of a human boy.

I know what they are. I can see it in the mirror.

They are the eyes of a dragon.

"But I can't be a dragon," I say. Looking up at the

glass dragon, I step back and spread my arms to show it what I am. "I'm . . . I'm a boy."

The bells ring in the dragon's voice again. *Can you not see what you are?*

I look down at myself. I'm the son of Jos By-the-Water, and I'm homesick for my village, and worried about it, too. I have one shoe off and one shoe on. I'm wearing the ordinary clothes that Maud gave me. My human heart is banging away in my chest, my hands are trembling until I have to grip the mirror so that I don't drop it. But the spark inside me. It's burning hotter than ever.

"How?" I whisper. "How can I be a dragon?"

Come, the glass dragon says, getting up and uncurling its tail from around its hoard of lenses. It rests its fore-claw on the ground and turns it. After putting the mirror back with the rest of the hoard, I climb on and it holds me around the middle; there's a rush of wind, and it lifts from the floor. A thunder of wings, and a moment later we land on the rim of the Ur-Lair. From far away it looks like the edge of a teacup. When I climb out of the glass dragon's claw, I find that the rim is ten feet wide, covered with broken rock. The other dragons fly up, too, and land, all perched in a line along the rim like a row of huge, colorful birds.

The Ur-Lair is behind me. The sky is a clear blue

bowl overhead. From here I can see that a morning mist is lifting from the folds of forested, snow-dusted hills below me. The faint line of the road leads out of the hills and away over a distant plain. The air is icy cold and the wind blows hard, making me stagger, and then I brace myself against the glass dragon's leg. Its scales are warm and smooth under my hand.

It turns its huge head and looks down at me.

When I speak, my words are snatched away by the wind. "Are you going to turn me into a dragon?"

You already are a dragon, it tells me.

"How?" I shout.

It looks outward again. *Fly*, it says.

I gulp. "You want me to jump?"

No, the glass dragon says. *Fly.*

Carefully I step to the edge and look down. The side of the mountain is steep, bare rock and ash, with snow lower down where it can cling to the slopes. And below that, the dark tree line.

Next to me, the indigo dragon snorts. *A long way down*, it says. *Squishy boy will fall on the rocks. Make a mess.*

It *is* a long way down.

See, says the glass dragon, and points with a claw.

I turn to look. Far below us there's a puff of black smoke. Faintly, on the wind, I hear the rattle and clash of a steam engine. And then Gringolet's convoy emerges from the trees and onto the road leading up the side of the mountain. First comes the big vapor-wagon that is crowded with men. Then comes the huge canvas-covered mystery machine pulled by two more vaporwagons.

There is no time, the dawn-pink glass dragon says. *You must see what you truly are. You must decide* now. *Fly.*

So I take a deep breath, and I say goodbye to Rafi Bywater . . .

. . . and I jump.

CHAPTER 30

I remember the day when Gringolet and Stubb first came to my village, and I was up on the Dragonfell and wanted to leap off it, into the wind. If I had jumped that day, would I have turned into a dragon? Has my dragon self been waiting all this time?

Or would I have plummeted down off the Dragonfell and died on the rocks below?

I fall from the edge of the Ur-Lair. The steep, ashy gray walls of the mountain flash past, and the wind howls in my ears.

My body feels heavy, like a stone, falling straight down. Sparks gather around me, streaming away in the wind of my fall.

The rocky slope gets closer. Closer.

I shut my eyes. The wind buffets me, and I tumble, head over heels, and any second I expect it all to end, for the earth to pull me into it. Then time slows, just as it did when the Coaldowns dragon held me under its claw. Between one tick of a pocket watch and the next, the sparks around me burst into flames. I burn as I fall; I am a shooting star, I'm a comet, I'm a bolt of lightning. My skin and bones and muscles burn away. My head goes down again, and I tumble, and when I come around again, my wings open with a mighty clap, and my whole body jerks as I tell the earth *No, you can't have me yet.* My eyes pop open and I see the ashy rocks of the mountain just a foot below me, and a second later I'm soaring away on wide, wide wings.

I am fierce, powerful. My muscles shift under my burning-hot scales. Testing my wings, I bank and soar higher. I give my tail a twitch, and it pushes the wind away, and I change direction. The air feels thick, solid, holding me up, almost like water.

High above, I can see the other dragons, all lined up on the rim of the Ur-Lair, watching.

My mouth opens, and I shout out a roar of joy. I am a *dragon*! At the sound, rocks tremble, and swags of snow slide down into the tree line.

And then my keen eyes see a small shape climbing the side of the mountain toward the Ur-Lair. It's Maud.

I can see that she is shaking with cold, and her hands are scraped and bloody, and she is limping. But she is still coming. Then she straightens and looks up at me, shading her eyes with her hand to see better.

She is my Maud, and that means I know exactly what she is doing. Her friend Rafi was taken away by a dragon, so she is going to rescue him.

Also she's a scientist of dragons, so she wants to see them up close. Well, she's about to get her chance.

I angle my wings and lower my tail, and go into a dive.

Seeing me, Maud shrieks and falls to the ground, curling into a ball with her arms over her head.

As I swoop over her, I reach down with a claw and snatch her up, cradling her gently, like an egg, holding her against my chest to keep her warm so the icy air doesn't freeze her. I point my snout at the top of the mountain and pump my wings, gaining height effortlessly, until I glide over the rim of the Ur-Lair. Almost lazily I spiral down to the stone floor. The other dragons follow, making a circle around me.

Carefully, I set Maud on the ground. She's curled up tight, still holding her arms over her head. "Is it really you, Rafi?" she asks, her voice muffled. Trembling, she peers out at me.

How did she *know*!?

And then I realize. Maybe she's *always* known.

I can't talk to her in this shape. I reach out and poke her with the tip of a claw.

She gets to her feet, and I can see how hard she's shaking with cold and with fright. She clasps her hands together and looks around at all the other dragons, then gazes up at me, her eyes wide. "Oh my g-goodness," she murmurs. "It really is you."

The little human is cold, says one of the heads of the two-headed blue dragon.

Give it some hoard, says the other.

They take off one of their knitted hats and drop it onto Maud's head.

She *meeps* because it's so big that it covers her face, and then peers from under it as the knitter dragon takes a scarf from one of its necks and, crouching gingerly, holds it out to her.

"Thank you," Maud says, and with shining eyes she takes the scarf and wraps it around her. Both the hat and the scarf are made of blue yarn, and they look like they will keep her warm. Then she steps closer to me and rests a hand on my leg, and I realize how big I am. I am not huge like the glass dragon; I'm not even as big as the Coaldowns dragon. For a dragon, I am little, but for a Rafi, I am enormous, taller than any man. Maud doesn't even come up to my wings. My scales are ember-bright, the same color as my hair. I crane my head to look over my shoulder, and see wings that blaze like fire, and a long tail that ends in wicked spikes. I can feel the white-hot molten heat inside me, too. It's hotter than any coal-fired steam engine. My spark burns hotter than all the other dragons' sparks. If I wanted to, I could open my mouth and breathe out flames, and they would turn everything they touch into ash.

"You're so, so beautiful, Rafi," Maud says. She takes a ragged breath. "I had a feeling, you know." Then she gives me such a Maud-like look, bright-eyed and curious. "It was the goats."

I cock my head. The goats?

"All the goats," she goes on, "following you anywhere you go." She smiles up at me. "They're coming here now, aren't they?"

They are, I know it. I miss them, and I hope they catch up to me soon.

She leans against my shoulder. "The goats are your hoard." A laugh bubbles up in her throat. "A herd-hoard. There's no precedent. I mean, I've never read anything that said a person could be a dragon at the same time, but seeing you with the goats, that made me suspect what you really are." And then she does the most Maud-like thing she's ever done, which is to dig through the scarf covering her to reach into her pocket and pull out her dragon notebook. "Rafi," she says. "I think I've figured out why Mister Flitch wants your spark." She looks around at all the dragons. "And what he's really been collecting from the dragons that he's killed." From the back of her book she takes a folded piece of paper. "Look. Can you understand this?" she asks, kneeling and spreading it on the stone floor.

I crouch and peer at it, and it's as much a blur to my dragon eyes as it was to my human ones. I snort out a frustrated puff of smoke. And then I remember what the Skarth dragon said to me. *Rafi sees far, cannot see to read.* The Skarth dragon had tiny spectacles on a chain.

I get to my clawed feet and face the glass dragon, who has flown down with the rest of the dragons to crouch nearby.

Can I borrow one of your hoard? I ask.

As an answer, it holds out a pair of spectacles, just the right size for a very large person or a somewhat small dragon. I take them into my claw and try putting them on, but they tip off and fall, and Maud only just manages to dive and catch them before they shatter on the stone floor of the Ur-Lair.

"Here," she says, standing and polishing the lenses on the knitted scarf. "Let me try."

I lower my head and she stretches up and balances the spectacles on my snout. I look through them, at the paper that Maud spread out on the floor, and it comes perfectly into focus.

Maud edges closer. "Rafi, I was planning to show this to you this morning," she says quietly. "I . . . Well, I lied to you about Mister Flitch's workroom in the factory. I didn't want you to think that I knew too much about it, but I have been into it before, and I have seen the machines that he's been building. Back then I drew a picture of them, and I kept it in my notebook. I figured they must be another kind of factory machine, but now I know that they're not. I thought you might be able to make sense of it."

It's a diagram. Yes, I know how this works. Gears, pistons, cylinders.

Yes, it's a machine.

Maud can't see it, but I can: when it is powered up, it will unfold and expand into the shape . . .

. . . into the shape of a dragon.

It is made of gears and pistons, with polished iron talons and sharpened metal teeth.

Maud is crouched next to me. "Look," she says, pointing at the diagram. "There's no coal box, no steam engine." She glances up at me. "What is powering it?"

I peer closely at the drawing of Flitch's mechanical dragon. Maud is right. It's not powered by a coal fire. It's powered by a flame of a different kind.

I know—now I know what Flitch really wants with the dragons, and with me. For him, our dragon flame is *useful*. Even better than coal.

I rear back and open my maw and let out a ferocious roar. The sound echoes like thunder from the mountain.

I'm aware of Maud curled on the ground with her arms over her head again.

Sorry about that, Maud, I want to tell her.

And then I open my wings with a thunderous clap and leap into the sky, because Gringolet is here to collect a dragon's spark—to kill a dragon and steal its flame—to power one of Mister Flitch's machines.

And, oh, I am going to stop her.

CHAPTER 31

My wings buffeting the air, I climb out of the crater and fly over the rim of the mountain.

Below, halfway up the ashy side of the Ur-Lair, is Gringolet's convoy.

With a flap of my wings, I soar away from the mountain, then dive down to get a better look.

The lead vaporwagon is driven by Gringolet. She sees me coming, and shrieks, jumps out of the wagon, and hides underneath it like a bug scuttling under a rock. The men in the back scatter, some of them drawing weapons, others trying to hide among the rocks.

I fly lower and as I turn, I pass over the canvas-wrapped shape on the cart pulled by two vaporwagons. With my claw I slice right through the canvas, which falls away to reveal Mister Flitch's mechanical dragon, all hunched and gleaming in the morning light. It holds no fire—it is a dead thing, only metal with no spark.

Gringolet was coming to the Ur-Lair to kill the glass dragon and steal its spark for this false dragon.

I bank and feel my flame burning hotter than ever—it's stoked with all of my fury and sorrow—and I open my maw and my fire flows out, engulfing the machine.

I know why Flitch wanted me, even more than these other dragons. Their sparks do not burn as hot as mine. With my flame he could power all of his factories and an army of mechanical dragons.

I hover, bathing the false dragon in my fire, until its gears and rods and pistons glow white-hot and they slump and drip, melting into a useless metal lump.

And then I swoop into the sky, roaring out my triumph. From far below, I can hear Gringolet's men shrieking with fright as they flee down the mountain.

I go into a dive, straight toward where Gringolet is hiding. Gringolet, who could have been a dragon, but chose otherwise. Banking, snow swirling around me, I settle onto the ground.

She crawls out from under one of the vaporwagons. She's bony and stiff, and glinting with pins, and she's lost her smoked-lens spectacles, and I can see how her eyes once had a spark in them, but they're dead now. When she gave up that spark, what she really lost was herself. Straightening, she brushes snow off her front, then puts her hands on her hips and looks me up and down.

Then she nods. "So you've made your choice, Rafi Bywater."

I have, I say, even though I know she can't understand me. I want to ask her if she regrets her choice. But I think I already know the answer.

"You do burn brightly," she says bitterly. "I knew you would. Once we found you in that backwater village of yours I told Flitch that we should go after you before you realized what you are." Then she shrugs. "But it doesn't matter. You're too late."

Too late?

As if she understands my question, she nods. "You might want to ask yourself two questions," she says dryly. "Flitch isn't here. Where is he?" Then she points at the melted ruins of the mechanical dragon. "That's one of his machines. The other one has my spark in it. Where is it?"

A bolt of fright spears through me. I have no more time for Gringolet. Leaving her, I leap into the air and fly back to the Ur-Lair, spiraling to the floor inside, where Maud is waiting.

Flitch! I say to the glass dragon as I land with a *thump* on the stone floor near its hoard of lenses and mirrors. *He has built two false dragons. Where is the other one?* I ask the glass dragon. *Can you see?*

The glass dragon reaches into the chest that holds its hoard and pulls out a ball-shaped glass. *See*, it says. *Look into the glass and see.*

I crouch so Maud can put on my spectacles again, and I peer into the glass ball. It's cloudy at first, and then it clears.

It will show you your lair, the glass dragon murmurs from nearby. *The place of your heart, Rafi of Dragonfell.*

And it does. The clouds part, and I see the high fells, deep in snow now that winter has begun. And below it, my village.

But I barely glance at it, because coming up the road from Skarth is a vaporwagon, its smoke staining the air. Two other vaporwagons are pulling carts, and on the carts is a huge shape wrapped in canvas.

It's the mechanical dragon—and this one is powered by a real dragon's spark.

Flitch is bringing destruction to my village.

Without wasting a second, I grab Maud, and ignoring her questions and protests, I hurl myself into the sky and head for home.

Flitch knows that I will do anything to protect Dragonfell—my lair. The horror of what he might do to my village shivers through me. I imagine cottages burning, dead sheep everywhere, Old Shar fleeing in terror, my da trying to run from the mechanical dragon.

I'm an arrow, all speed, holding Maud with both claws clutched to my chest, and I leave a fiery wake behind me.

I'm too late. I know it.

As I fly, the hills below us unroll into the flat plain, and the Ur-Lair mountain recedes into the distance. A dark smudge on the horizon is Skarth. My keen dragon eyes catch a glimpse of hundreds of factory chimneys belching black coal smoke into the sky. Then I turn and head toward the fells. Pumping my wings, I climb from the valley and see the bare, snow-covered hills, and the road from Skarth, which has been cleared of snow. Deep ruts are scraped into it. And then I see something that makes my flame burn hot with fury. A line of vaporwagons loaded with coal, heading *away* from the Dragonfell.

And *there*. More coal smoke where it shouldn't be.

I hurtle past my village, and I see that the cottages are still standing, and then I see it—a coal mine.

Mister Flitch offered me a choice, and I didn't take it. He told me that if he couldn't have my flame he'd take what he needed from under my village. He needs power—he's doing exactly what he said he'd do: he's digging coal from under the Dragonfell.

The mine is halfway up the Dragonfell. A road leading

to it has been hacked out of the rocky side of the fell. The mine itself is a wide, deep pit, and an immense metal scaffold supports a mining machine that is hard at work, digging into the fell, sending up clouds of black smoke, spitting out rocks and shards that workers are shoveling up and carting away to pile in mullock heaps not far away. There's a crust of black coal dust over the snow all around the mine. Vaporwagons with black smoke swirling around them are lined up, waiting to be filled with coal for the factories in Skarth. There's another engine that pumps water out of the mine and down the center of the village street; the water steams and gives off a smell like rotten eggs. There are canvas tents, and fires burning. Waiting near the mine entrance is an enormous, canvas-covered shape on a wagon—Mister Flitch's mechanical dragon.

I bank sharply, and as I turn I see the workers screaming and shouting and pointing up at me, and people running out of the tents.

Folding my wings, I plunge toward the ground, where I land only for a second, long enough to set Maud down, and then I leap into the air again. As I flash by, I catch a glimpse of the workers. Jeb and Jemmy stand by a cart full of broken rock, and I see Tam Baker's-Son, who has been picking up shards of mine tailings, and I see Old Shar bent under the load of rocks she's carrying on her back. They all stare, and I see Tam gaping. I don't see my da anywhere. I hope he is safe.

Maud knows what I am here to do—I will destroy the coal mine engine and send Mister Flitch and his men back where they came from. I will protect my village.

Maud has flung off the knitted hat and scarf, and she's already shouting and waving her arms, telling the workers to get away from the mine. I climb higher and see men running away from the engine, abandoning it. Other workers are streaming from the mouth of the mine itself.

The fire builds inside me, boiling hotter with my fury. I climb higher, past the very top of the Dragonfell, the lair where the first dragon kept a hoard of blue-painted teacups. Then I turn and aim myself at the mining engine.

At the same moment, there is a roar from the huge, canvas-wrapped shape on the cart near the mine entrance.

I am ready—I have been expecting it.

The canvas splits along its seams, ripping away to reveal a machine that gleams with its own wicked light. It unfolds, lifting itself off the cart with a shrieking of metal and a grinding of gears. Clouds of poisonous steam erupt, and when they clear, it emerges.

The mechanical dragon.

It is far, far bigger than I am. It is powered by Gringolet's dragon spark—and by the sparks stolen from the bell dragon, and from fifty dragon-flies, and from the teacup-collecting dragon who used to lair here. Wreathed in steam, it is all metal and gears and rivets, with four piston-driven legs and a whirling mass of blades at its tail end. Molten heat radiates from its metal skin. A giant head appears, swiveling back and forth as if it's looking for something. As I swoop closer, its jaw creaks open, and it roars out a blast of heat and steam that slams into me, sending me crashing into the side of the fell with my wings crumpled beneath me. Righting myself, I catch a glimpse of the mechanical dragon's chest, where there's a thick, curved window. Inside it I can see Mister Flitch. He's pulling levers and pushing buttons—he's driving the dragon.

As I launch myself back into the air, the dragon-engine looms above me, clouding the air with soot and shadow. Gears roar as it pulls back its head to strike. A gob of flaming, stinking tar bursts from its maw and arcs toward me.

I am small, for a dragon, but I am fast. With a flick of my wings I dart out of the way, and the fireball of burning tar splatters onto the rocks behind me. A pump of my wings, and I swoop past the dragon-engine, open my mouth, and spray it with a blast of furious fire. My flames are repelled by the engine's metal skin. Inside it Mister Flitch throws a lever, and the engine's flail-like tail strikes out at me. I dodge, but not fast enough, and the whirling blades slice into my flank. Roaring with the pain of it, I tumble, head over wings over tail, and slam into the ground. All around, people are screaming and running away and hiding.

I get to my clawed feet, my tail lashing with fury, feeling blood dripping from my wound. I shake the mud and snow off my wings.

The dragon-engine stalks toward me, its every footstep shaking the ground. Through the window on its chest I can see Mister Flitch sneering down at me. He reaches over his head to turn a dial, then slams his fist on a button. In response, the engine's mouth opens, and scalding steam blasts out.

But I am already gone. I fling myself into the air, where it cannot follow, and aim myself at the mineworks. With the dragon-engine lumbering after me, I blast the mine-digging engine with my hottest fire. Its metal scaffold sags. I bank and make another pass, slicing at it with my claws, and the entire structure tilts, and with a high-pitched scream of tortured metal, it falls like an enormous tree, crashing into the snow and soot-covered ground.

I shout out a roar of triumph, but the dragon-engine has already turned. Clouds of black smoke billow from its mouth as it heads away from the destroyed mine.

Toward my village.

CHAPTER 32

The dragon-engine thunders toward the village, and I speed after it, as fast as my wings can take me, trailing sparks and drops of blood from the wound on my flank. It rumbles down the main street, past Old Shar's rebuilt cottage, past the bakery and the forge, and I see where Flitch is going.

Toward my da's cottage, at the very edge of the village.

Desperate, I streak past the dragon-engine, and let loose a stream of fire that scorches it from head to tail.

It lumbers on.

I bank sharply and dive at it, dragging my claws across its back. Blue sparks fly up, but its metal skin is not even marked. Just in time, I catch a glimpse of its flail-tail barreling toward me, and I fling myself out of the way, and it slams into the ground like a boulder.

A grinding of gears, and the dragon-engine goes on.

And then I see something that makes my heart shiver in my chest.

Maud, running as fast as she can down the center of the road. She runs practically under the dragon-engine's belly, and a moment later she is through the gate in the stone wall around my da's cottage. When she gets to the front door, she turns and braces herself in the doorway. As if her own small human body can provide any defense against the massive engine that her father has built.

Her face is wild and desperate, and she's looking up at the dragon-engine, and I know that Mister Flitch—her father—is staring back at her.

Slowly the engine's head draws back. Its maw cranks open. A billow of black steam leaks out.

In the doorway, Maud squeezes her eyes shut. She is shaking like a leaf in the wind, but she doesn't get out of the way.

He is going to do it. Flitch is going to kill his own daughter.

I was angry before, but now I am past fury, into a white-hot flame of destruction. The feeling builds in me, and builds, and I hurl myself into the air, my wings stroking until I reach the top of my dive. As I turn in the air, I fold my wings and I become a bolt of white-hot lightning, and I aim myself at the dragon-engine's heart. As I spear through it the air crashes behind me with a thunder that shakes the ground and echoes from the fells all around.

Because I studied the vaporwagon, I understand how this mechanical dragon works. I know just where to aim my fire so that it will be destroyed.

As I flash past the dragon-engine, my mouth opens, and the flame of my fury is a spear of light that smashes into the engine, and this time it's hot enough and powerful enough to pierce the metal skin. The bolt finds the dragon-engine's heart—the sparks of many dragons hunted by Flitch and Gringolet, and killed by them, too. As my flame strikes the sparks, they burn together for half a second with the fire of the sun, and then, in a flash, they go dark.

The mechanical dragon groans, metal on metal, and a sound rips out of it, a roar like a factory engine pushed too hard and about to explode. The air is thick with soot and steam. The dragon-engine's head arches back, and back, over-cranked, and it rises onto its hind legs. There's a shrieking of gears, and a tearing of metal, and it tips over, landing with an echoing crash that shakes the ground.

I land on the road and whip my head around to check the door of the cottage.

It is open. My da is standing there with his hand on Maud's shoulder. They are both staring at me, and then beyond me to the shattered wreckage of the dragon-engine.

I see Maud say something to my da, who stares at me, his eyes wide, and then Maud leaves the doorway. I think she's running to me, and then she's past, her feet slipping on the snow and mud, to the steaming corpse of the dragon-engine.

"Help me, Rafi!" she calls.

The engine is a ruin of twisted metal and smashed pistons. Tendrils of acrid steam leak from burst seams. Maud climbs over it, to what is left of the engine's main section. The window has shattered. Among the shards of glass and the cracked dials and broken levers, lies Mister Flitch. He is pale, and his eyes are closed.

Maud crouches beside him. A plate of metal and rivets lies across his chest. She reaches out to shift it, then jerks back. It's too hot. It must be burning her father. "Rafi, quick, come help me get him out."

To dragon me, the metal plate weighs nothing, so I lift it away and toss it aside. I'm aware of my da limping out of our cottage. With Maud's help, I drag Mister Flitch out of the wreckage and onto the road. My da holds out a blanket, a fine wool one that he wove himself, and Maud darts to him, takes it, and runs back to cover her father with it.

And then Mister Flitch opens his eyes. With Maud's help, he sits up. His clothes, I realize, are fireproof and armored. The destruction of his dragon-engine left him only slightly injured. Pushing my da's blanket away, he gets to his feet.

The other villagers gather, murmuring and staring at me. I see Tam Baker's-Son, and Jeb and Jemmy, and I see Lah Finethread cast me a glance and then lean over and whisper something to John the Smith, who nods.

Then Mister Flitch coughs, drawing everyone's attention to himself. Maud gazes up at him with wide eyes, the same green as his eyes, which are narrowed as they study me.

"So," he says sharply. "The dragon has returned." He spares a glance for the villagers. "Just as I said it would. And it has destroyed the mine on which the entire village depends."

As Mister Flitch speaks, his men come down the road from the village. I see Stubb armed with a metal rod, and other men holding weapons. For a moment they look as if they might do something stupid, like attack the villagers, or come after me.

To dragon me they look small, like they're at the

other end of a long tunnel. I am fierce and powerful, and I could easily open my mouth, blast them with fire, and incinerate them all.

But just because I *can* doesn't mean that I *should*.

Instead I snort out a puff of smoke and give them a fierce glare. It's enough that they lower their weapons.

"Ah! It is just as I warned," Mister Flitch declares. "Beware! The dragon is evil and dangerous!"

At his words the villagers, the people I love best in the world, back away, their eyes wide. They are not frightened of Mister Flitch or his men, they are afraid of *me*.

And I can't even explain.

Dragons don't get tired easily. Flames can't burn us, cold doesn't affect us. We are strong. Even the pain of the wound on my flank barely bothers me.

But this hurts with an ache that settles in my heart. It hurts me worse than any weapon that Mister Flitch could build.

"Oh my *goodness*." Maud's hands are clenched into fists, and she stands in front of her father, glaring at him. Then she shifts her glare to the villagers. "It's not an evil dragon, it's *Rafi*. Can't you see that?"

"It's not Rafi! It's a dragon!" Lah Finethread answers, and the others nod, agreeing. "It wants to destroy the village!"

"Oh, he does *not*," Maud says, as if she's all out of

patience. "How can you be so stupid? Rafi is a dragon. Just because he's different doesn't mean he's dangerous! This is his lair, and he will protect it with his life. That is what dragons *do*." And then she pulls her trusty red notebook out of her pocket. "I," she announces, "am not only Mister Flitch's daughter, I am a dragon scientist." Seeing the villagers' confused looks, she adds, "That is a person who knows all that there is to know about something, and in this case, it is dragons." She hands the red notebook to the nearest person, who happens to be Old Shar. "Tell me, old woman," Maud says grandly. "Is this not the notebook of a dragon scientist?"

Old Shar blinks and then raises her eyebrows and opens the book. She studies the page as if she is reading, but I see her sneak a glance in my direction.

I know what she sees. A young dragon not much bigger than a tall man. His scales burn with the color of flames. His wings are battered from the fight with the dragon-engine, and he has a wound on his flank that drips with blood. And his eyes. She should know his eyes, shadow dark with a spark deep within them.

Old Shar snaps the book closed. "Miss Flitch is absolutely correct," she says briskly. "She is an expert on dragons, and this dragon is Rafi. *Our* Rafi."

The villagers mutter with surprise, but they don't look convinced.

"Whether he is *your Rafi* or not," Mister Flitch puts in smoothly, "the fact remains that the world has changed." His sharp eyes survey the villagers. "The world no longer needs dragons. It needs factories, and coal to run them, and people to work in them."

My da is still standing at the gate leading to our cottage. Now he hobbles out to the road, leaning heavily on his crutch. He does not so much as look at me. He nods at Mister Flitch. "That may be so," says my da, who isn't used to speaking up in front of this many people. But he speaks clearly, so everyone can hear him. "But there's no cloth so fine as the cloth I weave. And," he goes on, as the villagers nod in agreement, "there are no smiths who make weather vanes as well as our John Smithy, and there are no sheep that give wool stronger or lighter than Old Shar's longpelts do."

"That's right," somebody says, and I see nods all around.

Da takes a deep breath and goes on. "And there are no cheese creamier than the cheese Lah makes, and there are no shepherd dogs bred better than the ones Ma Steep raises."

More nods and murmurs of agreement.

"So I'm thinking, Mister Flitch," Da says, "that you can keep your mines and your factories. We're not cogs and pistons up here on the fells. We're not parts for keeping the machines running."

Mister Flitch is scowling. His men grumble and lift their weapons again. I narrow my eyes, and tense my muscles, ready to fight.

Then Maud steps up and points at Mister Flitch. "This man," she announces to everyone in the village, "is my father, and I know him better than anybody. He doesn't want to help anyone here. All he wants is power. Coal power, or a spark to drive his machines, because that gives him gold, and more gold, and another kind of power.

"There is a book," Maud goes on loudly. She glances at Old Shar. "I think you may have seen it. It was supposedly written by a person named Ratch. There's a line from that book that tells about a certain kind of creature who is"—and she quotes the Ratch book from memory—"*destructive, sly, thievering, greedy, foul, unnatural, selfish, contemptible, parasitical, and an entirely treacherous beast.*"

She glares at Mister Flitch.

"The words in Ratch's book do not describe dragons, Father," she shouts. "They are describing *you!*"

She turns her anger on the villagers. "Now, listen, you people. Which one of these would you rather have protecting you?" She points at her father. "Mister Flitch, who is turning your village into a coal mine and who has shown himself to be a *treacherous beast*?" And then she points at me, and the entire village is looking, maybe seeing me as I really am for the first time. "Or will you choose Rafi? This village is his lair—it is the place of his heart, and he will protect it, and the people who live here, with his life. So choose, people of Dragonfell. Which will you have?"

CHAPTER 33

The Ratch book said that dragons are evil, malicious creatures that turn all the land around them to waste.

When the villagers insist that Mister Flitch leave the Dragonfell, his men leave a waste behind them. Poisoned water, and a gaping pit in the side of the fell, and broken machinery.

The villagers are happy to have him gone, along with his men and his coal mine.

They chose me, but still, they're not so certain sure about me.

I am a dragon. So I go to my lair, high atop the Dragonfell. I settle there among the shards of blue-painted teacups that the first dragon hoarded. From that spot I have a good view of the vaporwagons leaving the village, trundling down the road toward the valley. I can see what's left of the mine and the heaps of slickens where sheep used to graze. They'll graze there again, I think, once spring comes.

Maud climbs the fell to say goodbye. She's going back to Skarth to deal with her father, she tells me. To put things right. "He's not a good man," she says. "But he didn't kill me when he had the chance. So it could be worse." And that's one of the things I love best about Maud. She'll always find something to be cheerful about. But then she frowns. "I'll have to get rid of his dragon collection. If he gives me any trouble, I will let you know, Rafi, and you can come and set him straight. And I'll make sure the other dragons are resettled in their lairs, and left undisturbed."

I don't have any doubt that she'll manage all of it. She is a dragon scientist, after all.

Maud sighs, leaning against my flank and admiring the view from my lair. "Rafi, you're the best friend I'll ever have," she says with a contented sigh. "I'm going to miss you."

I'm going to miss her, too.

"I'll probably come back in a few weeks," she goes on. "Once I get things settled in Skarth." She rolls her eyes. "My father is a very smart man, you know, but he is very stupid about some things. And I was thinking . . ."

If I was a boy, I would laugh at that. Maud thinking is when things get dangerous.

She casts me a sidelong look, as if she knows that I'm laughing inside my head. "No, seriously, Rafi, I have an idea. Your friend Old Shar isn't wrong. Things *are* changing. There are factories, and vaporwagons, and they run on coal, and the thing is, coal mines make a terrible mess, and the smoke from coal-burning engines makes a mess, too. What if there's a way for dragons to . . . I don't know, to *lend* part of their spark to make those things run, instead of coal? It wouldn't be like Mister Flitch *taking* your spark, you'd be *giving* it, just a tiny piece of it. It would be different."

Trust Maud to come up with an idea like that.

"Think about it while I'm gone," Maud says brightly. Then she gives me a brilliant grin. "And I know you won't be lonely."

Yes, I will.

She points, and I can't believe she saw them first. Coming up the path from the village is a line of goats. The billy goat, Gruff, is leading them, and Poppy and Elegance, and all the others, even the babies Cloud and Coal. The sight of them fills me with a deep feeling of rightness. My hoard.

"Oh, and there's one more thing, before I go." Maud reaches into her pocket and takes out my spectacles, which she sets on the rock beside me. Then she takes out the dragon book and waves it at me. "I have to take this back so the Skarth dragon can add it to its library hoard. But I read something important that I have to tell you about." She pats my leg. "It's like standing next to a furnace, Rafi. I can see why you'll never get cold up here. Anyway, I finished reading the book, and I know all the dragon secrets now. And the best one is how the dragon-touched can be a dragon, and how he can be a person, too." She gazes up at me, her eyes shining, and then she tells me how.

The next morning, the boy named Rafi heads down from the dragon's lair on the Dragonfell, followed by his hoard of goats. It snowed during the night, but I'm only wearing a ragged shirt and trousers, and no shoes. My human shape never fit me all that well, and it feels strange to be wearing it now. I can feel the flame that burns inside me. I never was a boy, really. I was a dragon who was stuck in his boy shape for his entire life, until he found out what he really was.

All dragons, Maud told me, are dragon-touched to start with, and have a human form. And then, when their human body gets very old, they stop being able to shift, and they stay in their dragon shape for the rest of their lives, which is a very long time. This must be true, because she read it in the dragon book.

The goats follow as I walk down the path, past the wreckage of the mine, and then past John Smithy's house. He's hard at work at his forge, banging away at something. Seeing me, he sets down his hammer and holds up the iron weather vane he's working on. It's a new design. It's shaped like a dragon, and it looks a lot like me.

I feel a wide grin break over my face. "If you ever need help getting the fire in your forge started," I call, "I can help with that. Just let me know!"

He blinks, and then nods. "I will, Rafi," he calls back. "Certain sure I will."

Still smiling, I continue on my way. In the middle of the road is a channel made by the water pumped out of the coal mine. There's a film over the water that's left in it, and a lingering smell of sulfur. When the snow melts, it'll wash it all away, I hope.

As I reach Old Shar's house, she comes out to meet me. She folds her arms and leans on her gate and looks me up and down. "Well now, Rafi."

"Good morning, Old Shar," I say politely, just like my da taught me. My voice sounds rough, like I've been gargling fire. Which I guess I have.

Old Shar fixes me with her sharpest look. "Schooling tomorrow," she says. "You *will* be coming, won't you?"

"Yep," I say. I can't wait to show her my reading spectacles, and tell her that I never was as stupid as I thought I was.

The goats catch up to me. *Maaah*, Poppy says, complaining about the mud and snow on the road. They don't like getting their hooves wet.

"You can leave the hoard in your lair when you come, Rafi," Old Shar says. "But you tell that delightful friend of yours, Maud, that she's welcome anytime." And then she turns and goes back into her house.

As I pass through the village, Tam peers at me from the doorway of his father's bakery. "Mornin', Rafi," he calls.

"Mornin'," I answer, and stop walking.

"Sorry about before," Tam says, coming to his gate. He's shivering a little in the icy wind. "Telling about you touching the fire with your hands, about what I saw that time."

I feel all wound up inside. "It's all right," I say.

"No, 'tisn't." He shakes his head. "I shouldn't have said it. But I was thinking just the same." He glances quickly up at me, then away. "I was thinking," he goes on slowly, "that it would be useful."

Tam looks ready to run away screaming if I so much as twitch, so I hold myself very still. "Useful?" I repeat.

"Yes. Not getting burned. For a baker especially. My

da has burns all over." Tam pulls up his shirtsleeve and shows a healing burn on his wrist. "I got that one when I brushed up against the bread oven, and I was thinking, maybe I should touch you for luck. To keep me safe from being burned."

I blink, surprised. "I don't think that'll work," I tell him.

"Might as well try it." He opens the gate and crosses the road to me, and holds out his hand, and he only flinches a little when I take it in mine. "It feels funny," he says.

Different. Strange. I know.

"It's like . . ." He wrinkles his nose, thinking. "It's like when a loaf of bread comes out of the oven. When it's cooling, you can touch it on the crust, but on the inside it's still hot and steaming." He lets go of my hand.

"So . . . I'm like bread," I say.

Tam offers me a corner of a smile. "Well, you're more like a dragon, Rafi."

And that's all right? Are we friends again? Is that what Tam is saying?

"See you tomorrow at Old Shar's house for school," he says, and hurries back inside the warm bakery.

"Huh," I say, and I go on down the road until I get to my da's cottage.

From out on the road, I can hear the *swath* and *whirr*

and *thump-thump* of Da's loom. When I get to the gate and open it, the sound of the loom goes quiet.

I stand there, half afraid to go in. I have so much to tell my da. He's always been afraid of fire, and afraid of dragons, and that's what I am. I don't think I can stand it if he's afraid of me, too.

The cottage door creaks open. Da stands there, leaning on his crutch. He looks thinner, as if he didn't get enough to eat while I was gone. His face is etched with the pain of his burned leg. For a long moment, he doesn't say anything. Then, "Rafi," he says, and his voice breaks on my name.

I stand there, half ready to run back to my lair on the Dragonfell.

Da looks at me, and I don't know what he's thinking. "There's something," he says slowly, "I've been meaning to tell you."

I nod.

"There's something that I fear more than fire," he says.

I nod again. I remember him saying that before, when I left the cottage. My heart drops. "Dragons," I say sadly, and I know how lonely I'm going to be without him. "You're afraid of dragons."

"No," Da says firmly. "That's not it. The one thing I fear more than anything, Rafi, the thing I've always been most afraid of, is losing you."

And then he opens his arms, and a second later I'm across the yard and standing on the doorstep before him, and his arms wrap around me in a hug, and I'm home, in my place, where I belong.

ACKNOWLEDGMENTS

Thanks to:

My BFFs, Jenn Reese, Deb Coates, and Greg van Eekhout.

And my dear pal Michelle Edwards.

To the team at HarperCollins Children's Books, especially Alyson Day.

To my agent, Caitlin Blasdell at the Liza Dawson Associates agency.

And to everybody who's a little bit dragon.